LEAP INTO DANGER

LEIF HAMRE

Seen from the air, the white-and-green beauty of the vast Norwegian forest hardly seemed a portrait of peril. Yet the moment the motor of their plane had failed, the two young Air Force pilots knew that the routine patrol had turned into a rendezvous with impending disaster.

The parachute descent into the frozen wilderness below is merely a prologue. Then begins their struggle for survival while a blizzard rages, preventing search planes from making a rescue operation. Their ingenious plans to keep alive—a rough shelter of branches, fishlines rigged through the ice in a nearby lake, and snares set for ptarmigan—at first help to sustain them.

But when—despite a roaring fire outside their flimsy shelter entrance—a pack of ravening wolves draws closer and closer, both men are filled with the chilling doubt that they will ever be found alive.

Leif Hamre, a lieutenant-colonel in the Norwegian Air Force, has written from first-hand knowledge a taut, absorbing, and authentic story that takes the reader into the very heart of danger.

Leap Into Danger

LEIF HAMRE

Leap Into Danger

TRANSLATED FROM THE NORWEGIAN BY EVELYN RAMSDEN

HARCOURT, BRACE AND COMPANY NEW YORK

First American edition
First published in Norway in 1957 by H. Aschehoug & Co.
under the title *Otter Tre To Kaller!*
Library of Congress Catalog Card Number: 59–12343

Printed in the United States of America

Contents

Leap Into Danger

One — Northwards

It was night.

The Air Force station on the south side of Bodö lay dark and silent. No plane was in action; the doors of the hangars were closed and very few lights were visible, only the scattered street lamps throwing their pale circles on the snow. As a contrast, the control tower stood out solitary and fully lighted to the north of the runway, shining like a giant lighthouse in the darkness. The control staff were not asleep, nor were the officers and men who were on duty in the Operations Room. They were in a central underground room from which no ray of light appeared. The two brains of the air base, the civil one high above the ground and the military one far below, were in constant communication with the outer world by night as well as by day.

But in the huts the air crew and the technicians slept the sleep of the just.

A few hours after midnight the silence was broken by a prolonged ringing somewhere in the camp.

R-r-r-r-r!

Geir Grand turned in his sleep and pulled the eiderdown up over his ears.

R-r-r-r!

Goodness—was it morning already? Geir, half awake, gazed out into the darkness through the slits between his eyelids and, still confused and sleepy, stretched out his hand to turn off the alarm clock. But before he touched it, he was fully awake and realized that the clock was innocent of all this noise. He switched on his bedside lamp, sprang out of bed, and caught up the telephone.

"Hello!"

"Is that Lieutenant Grand?"

"Yes!"

"This is the Operations Room. The officer on duty wishes to speak to you. One moment please—"

A new voice that Geir knew well took over. "That you Geir? Right. Get ready as quickly as you can. You are to take off for ambulance duty to Kirkenes half an hour before daybreak."

"Kirkenes?" said Geir, surprised. "A 'Norseman' from Tromsö could be there almost two hours before me!"

"Certainly! If we had one available. But they are all detailed to other jobs!"

"O.K. When is daybreak?"

"At 6:40!"

Geir glanced at the clock. It was a quarter past four. "Have you rung the technician on duty?"

"Yes, the plane will be clear in three-quarters of an hour. The kitchen was warned ten minutes ago. Breakfast will soon be ready."

"Fine! Let me have a jeep outside the mess in half an hour."

"Right—wait a moment! Your new Flight Sergeant hasn't flown an Otter. Are you taking him with you or shall I give you someone else?"

Geir started and turned round quickly.

"Death and destruction!" he exclaimed involuntarily. Peter Hovden, his new roommate,* was sitting on the edge of his bed gazing at him eagerly. He looked about seventeen—thin, freckled, of middle height, and with childish blue eyes, yellow curly hair, and a faint down on his chin. Geir could not, with the best will in the world, feel that this boy was one who inspired a feeling of great confidence—this, apart from the fact, that he himself had very little use for inexperienced airmen who had just come from training school and thought they were experienced if they could manage to keep a bus in the air.

"He must have falsified his birth certificate," thought Geir. "He's not dry behind the ears yet."

"Hallo! Are you there?" came over the telephone.

"Yes—I don't know what to say. The weather isn't too good up there, so that there ought to be two of us who know the route and the country—up to a point, at any rate!"

Peter's shoulders slumped; his excited expression died down and his eyes flickered uncertainly. His disappointment was so evident that Geir sighed resignedly.

* In the Norwegian Air Force, with which this story deals, commissioned officers, non-commissioned officers, and men all share sleeping quarters and mess together. This is not so in most military establishments.

"O.K.," he said, as if he were answering a question. He raised his voice. "I'll take him with me!"

"As you like. Ring if there's anything else you want. So long!"

"So long!"

Geir put back the receiver with a bang and pulled off his pajama top. He shivered, for it was raw and cold. Peter was still sitting on the edge of his bed looking at him questioningly.

"What are we—" he began.

"Into your clothes, boy!" Geir interrupted him crossly. "And be quick about it. We've got exactly ten minutes to dress!"

He pulled his shirt over his head and snapped, "Jump to it, boy! What are you gaping at?"

Peter started violently. He wriggled out of his pajamas and struggled into his undershirt and pants in a trice, his arms and legs waving in his efforts to be quick.

Watching him out of the corner of his eye while hastily dressing himself, Geir gave a half smile, but a moment later his irritation reasserted itself and he exploded again.

"Where the heck do you think we're going—to the Riviera?"

Peter straightened himself up, quite taken aback. "No, of course not. I thought I heard you say Kirkenes!"

"Then dress yourself accordingly," said Geir shortly. "We don't fly in undershirts and pants in the north of Norway in wintertime!"

"Oh, all right!" said Peter with a sigh. "I thought it was warm enough in the plane."

"Yes, of course it is. But it is quite possible you may find yourself outside the plane in the course of the trip."

Peter gave in. He dived into his trunk and began pulling out his winter underclothes.

Geir was already half dressed and was packing his toilet things in a small suitcase.

"Shaving must wait till later," he said, with a glance at Peter's downy chin. "That is to say, if you shave at all," he added.

"Twice a week," smiled Peter wryly, and bit his lip in an effort to refrain from answering sarcastically. It was true that he was a newly appointed sergeant, only just out of flying school, but more experience and his wings did not give Geir the right to treat him as a mere boy. Anyhow, Geir's wings were so bright that they could hardly be very old.

Peter pressed his lips together irritably but turned his head away from Geir to hide it. After all, he had probably flown the same types of plane as Geir—except, of course, the Otter. As if that needed any particular witchcraft!

Geir was ready. "You'll find me in the mess," he said. "Don't forget your toothbrush and leather jacket!"

The door slammed behind him. Peter pushed his unpleasant thoughts aside and hurried to get dressed. Either Geir's growling and grunting was his way of asserting his superior position or it was just morning grumpiness. He hoped it was the latter. In the mess when off duty he had been pleasant and easy, even if he was not exactly one of those who opened out to strangers and babbled about all that was in his mind. Actually Geir seemed a good deal older than he really was, his deep voice and his pipe being partly responsible for this impression, but not altogether. His steady gaze, his calm movements, and the confident way in which he spoke all bore witness to maturity and self-confidence. He was not particularly tall, but broad-shouldered and powerful. His face was rugged and clear-cut and framed by black, bristly close-cut hair, which stood up straight from his forehead like pigs' bristles.

"Exactly like pigs' bristles," thought Peter. It pleased him to have found something to criticize about Geir, something that spoiled the impression of unimpeachable correctness.

When Peter tumbled breathlessly into his seat in the mess, Geir was halfway through his breakfast. He had eaten two eggs and plenty of bacon and a couple of slices of bread. By the side of his plate lay five pieces of bread and butter in a heap, and he was buttering a slice between each mouthful, adding it to the pile.

"I'm buttering for us both," he said. "Get on with your breakfast. The car will be here"—he looked at the clock—"in twelve minutes."

The door opened and was then banged violently shut. A fair, broad-shouldered lieutenant, at least six feet tall, walked noisily across the floor in heavy boots. "He must use horse's hoofs as heel tips," thought Peter.

The new arrival shook his fist at Geir.

"You again!" he shouted, his voice vibrating through the room. "For the third time in three weeks a poor trembling bundle of nerves has been dragged out of his bed for your sake—just when five tortured hours of sleeplessness were merging into total oblivion!"

Geir laid down his knife and leaned back in his chair, smiling. Peter looked at him in astonishment. The expression on his face had completely changed; it was as if a mask had fallen off. Something in his eyes made it clear that a strong friendship existed between the two men. So he could be like that. Peter realized instinctively that Geir's intercourse with others was marked either by complete confidence or by—he didn't really know how to describe it—probably by complete indifference.

"Don't fuss until you see what I've ordered for your breakfast," said Geir. "Three eggs and five slices of bacon. Isn't that something to get up for?"

"Yes—if I can manage to get it down," answered his friend in a subdued voice. "I can't stand much. I have a nervous stomach!"

He stopped as he passed Peter and held out his hand.

"As far as my sleep-ridden eyes can see, you are a new acquaintance," he said. "I was christened Svein and have inherited the honorable family name of Rowan." Peter stood up. "My name's Peter Hovden," he said.

"Sit down, sit down," Svein said. "We don't bother about etiquette at night. The sergeants eat with the officers, although at dinner we've introduced the custom that the officers should eat sitting down and the sergeants standing up."

Geir shook his head, laughing.

"Oh, pipe down," he said. "The car will be here in a

couple of minutes and we've no time for any more nonsense. Give me another cup of coffee, Peter. I'll have a pipe while you finish."

Peter wondered why Svein had been alerted. He had his wings, so that he could not be a technician. Was he coming with them? Before he had made up his mind to ask, Geir said, "Svein flies helicopters. He was alerted with us so as to be ready in case anything should go wrong. He will sit in the helicopter quarters for an hour playing cards with his technician and then he'll go back to bed again!"

"Cards!" snorted Svein. "The technician and I sit opposite each other with the telephone between us—just waiting. As a matter of fact, as you've mentioned games—we need fresh blood in the table-tennis club. Do you play, Peter?"

"Yes, I've played a good deal," said Peter.

"Splendid! New experts are received with joy," said Svein, rubbing his hands together. "We haven't got many of them."

"Oh well—I'm not exactly an expert," said Peter carefully and met Svein's disconcerting glance.

"In that case you are playing fast and loose with the language," said Svein. "No one except experts 'plays' table tennis; the others just 'bash the ball about.' Real play only begins when the strokes have become reflex movements and the ball follows the course that thought indicates without troubling the brain with the manual work. The spinal cord and the arms hit the ball. One's brain maps out the strength and weakness of one's opponent and plans the counter moves. When one's study of one's opponent is complete and accurate, it is impossible to lose."

"Actually then you lose the last game," said Geir with a laugh.

"Nothing can be truer; that fits in perfectly with my theory," said Svein. "The fundamental weaknesses recur from day to day, but delicately shaded faults may change from time to time and must be studied when they turn up."

Geir winked at Peter. "Svein needs only four things in order to live," he said. "Helicopters, air, table tennis, and a little food."

"We must try out Peter this evening, Svein," he went on. "Just now we must drop this interesting topic as the car is waiting for us. If your stomach cannot take more than about eight or ten more slices of bread and butter and no one comes in for you to talk to, perhaps we shall see you in the Operations Room before we set off. So long!"

"So long!" said Svein.

Geir and Peter shivered as they pulled their pigskin jackets closer round their necks and emerged from the mess and sat down on the icy seats of the jeep.

"The Air Weather Office," said Geir to the driver.

It was pitch dark and 19 to 20° below freezing. The beams from the car lights were reflected back from the snow walls, which were about a yard high and ran along the sides of the runway. As far as they could see, the clouds lay fairly low, but at any rate the weather was fine.

It was warm and cozy in the Air Weather Office. The Weather Officer turned round from the table and nodded.

"You're up early!" he said.

"Too early!" said Geir. "What's the forecast?"

The officer pointed to the weather chart with his pencil. "Not particularly good," he answered. It's all right as far as Bardufoss, but it's pretty rough over the Finmark Moors. Low cloud and a strong wind, snow squalls, icing in the clouds and snow. I imagine you'll be above the clouds, about 8,000-9,000 feet, but it will be comparatively clear for coming down round Kirkenes. The whole of the Varanger Fjord district has a broken cloud-covering, but there is practically clear weather at Kirkenes itself, at any rate for the moment."

Geir sat down on a high stool and studied the weather chart for a time. "We shall keep below the clouds as far as Bardufoss at any rate," he said as he got up. "We shall have to look into the weather situation again when we get there while we're filling up. Thanks a lot."

They went to the Operations Room and drew up a plan of the flight.

"Good luck," said the Operations Officer. "It looks a bit murky."

"It'll be all right," said Geir. "The Otter'll make it all right, you'll see!"

When they came out to the jeep again, they heard the drone of the engines from the runway outside the hangar.

These were growling evenly and monotonously as they approached but roared full out as the jeep drew up beside the plane. The technician nodded from the side window, tested the magnetoes, and let the engine tick over.

"It's O.K.," he said when he came out. He handed the maintenance sheet to Geir who initialed it.

Geir looked at the time.

"We'll take off," he said. "Hop in, Peter; let's start!"

In the darkness the plane rolled slowly to the end of the runway and swung into the wind. The runway lights were switched on. Geir stopped, put on the brakes, ran the engine at full throttle, and tested the magnetoes. Then he eased the throttle back until the engine was just ticking over and pressed the radio button on the stick.

"Bodö control, this is Otter Three Two. Have I permission to take off for Bardufoss? Over."

The voice of the officer to whom they had submitted the plan of the flight came clearly and distinctly through the earphones. "Three Two, from Control. Clear for departure. The wind is northwest 15 knots. Good luck. Out!"

Geir hastily inspected the instrument panel, pushed the throttle as far forward as it would go, holding the brakes as he did so, and then he released them so suddenly that the plane leaped forward with a jerk. The runway lights came toward them two by two and then disappeared behind them—faster and faster.

Peter noticed with surprise that they left the ground long before he expected to do so. If the Otter was not exactly the smartest plane imaginable, it got off the ground quicker than most. He had never taken the air on such a short bit of runway before. They could not have rolled much more than a hundred yards, if that.

He looked at the altimeter. "We're climbing like a lift," he said into the microphone. "Are the tanks full?"

Geir nodded. He trimmed the rudder and took a wide rising swing out over the sea. They caught a glimpse of white-crested waves below them in the darkness. The coast lay like a gray-white strip to starboard, and a low line of lights marked out the main road to the north from Bodö.

Two — Mayday—Mayday!*

It was quite light when they got to Bardufoss. They swung in, landing in front of one of the hangars, and Peter gave a hand with filling up while Geir disappeared into the hangar to telephone the Air Weather Office. When he came back, the plane was serviced and ready, and Peter was in his place as second pilot. He opened the window and shouted, "Is it all right?"

"Fairly," answered Geir. He dug into his pipe with a match while he walked slowly round the plane, inspecting the rudder and the wings. As he passed Peter's window, he said, "Put the parachutes in their places on the seats."

"Are we to put them on?"

"Of course. We're going to fly above the clouds." Geir blew hard into his pipe once or twice, and it was obviously empty. A little later he blew again for no particular reason. While he stood there inspecting the ski-fitted fuselage, he felt absent-mindedly in his pockets for his tobacco pouch.

Peter, who had taken out the parachutes and put them in their places, had found Geir's tobacco pouch in the

* This is the international radio-telephone signal for SOS and originates from the French "m'aider" or "help me."

pilot's seat and brought it with him when he came out. Geir filled his pipe thoughtfully.

"We're waiting for a written weather report," he said. "I think it's coming along over there now!" He nodded in the direction of a soldier approaching on a bicycle.

A little later the cyclist dismounted beside Geir and handed him an envelope. It was the weather report, and the two men opened it and studied it together in silence.

"It doesn't look quite hopeless," said Peter. "Are we flying?"

"Yes," said Geir. He pulled a box of matches out of his pocket and walked toward the door. "Well, we'll be off!" he said.

Peter smiled. "Won't you have a smoke first?"

"Yes." Geir stopped. He went a little way from the plane and turned toward Peter with a rueful little smile, while he struck a match. "Yes—I meant to. Will you go in and see that everything is in order. I'll be with you in a minute."

The weather warning was soon confirmed. The farther they flew northeast, the darker and lower lay the clouds. In some places heavy patches of mist floated down the mountainsides and over the ridges, and Geir zigzagged between them. Peter positively sweated over the map. He had to keep a sharp lookout every time they swung round, for the plane was rocking and pitching so violently in the restless atmosphere that Geir himself had enough to do without following the course. After about three-quarters of an hour's flying, a dense snow shower blocked their way and forced them into an almost southerly course.

"We might as well go up now as later," said Geir.

Peter nodded. He was beginning to feel uneasy. They were flying toward a snow-covered mountain range that in places rose straight up into the gray cloud covering. The territory below them was rugged and slanted slightly upward in the direction in which they were flying. It was not an attractive landscape from an airman's point of view, grand and impressive in its way, but terrifyingly wild. For the first time Peter had an uneasy feeling that the ground was not always just something that lay below the airman and of which he was quite independent. Work up here, in this inhospitable part of Norway, undoubtedly made more demands on the airmen than did work farther south. This was a foretaste of the tasks that awaited him, and for some reason or other he felt security in the fact that it was Geir and none other sitting beside him, and that it was in Geir's company he was to gain the experience that was necessary before he began to fly his own plane.

"You can take over now," said Geir. "Give me the map and I'll work out a position from which we can start the navigation. Where are we now?"

Peter handed him the map and pointed with a little circling movement of his finger. He was not able to give the exact position, but it was enough for Geir. He spread the map out over his knees and gazed for a long time alternately at the map and out of the window. They were flying southeast along the Skibotten River. On the port side the snow showers shut out the view, and to the south the ground was partly hidden beneath low banks of cloud. Rivers and lakes were frozen and covered with snow and almost melted into one with the landscape itself.

Geir's eyes followed a little crooked strip in the snow. It started from the Skibotten River and wound southward to a great snow flat, which must be a lake. It might be the lake, he thought, that lay northwest of the Hellig Forest. Anyhow, it fitted in with Peter's indication of their position.

From a glance at the ground in front of them it became clear to Geir that this was not the moment to fix their position more particularly. It was more important to rise to a greater height. He drew a little ring on the map and nodded to Peter.

"Go up," he said. "Keep the course at 035 degrees until I get it worked out accurately."

Peter pushed the throttle from him and increased the speed. A moment later they plunged into a cloud. Everything around them turned gray and the windows were dim with moisture. The atmosphere was much more restless now, and Peter bent forward, working hectically, with his eyes glued to the instrument board. Now and again he looked at the window to see whether ice was forming. The engine throbbed evenly and monotonously. He checked on the tachometer and the air-speed indicator several times a minute and watched that the engine was not overheating. The altimeter turned slowly round and round.

Peter was surprised that Geir had turned over the blind flying to him, ignorant as he was of the Otter. But no doubt

Geir was trying him out. In a spare moment he caught Geir's eye and a quick nod of approval. He supposed it meant that the flying was going as it should. He could hardly expect much in the way of words or expressive glances from that quarter.

At 9,000 feet they emerged from the clouds. The sky was a clear blue and the sun was shining, and below them lay the clouds, arched and in rounded outlines like a mountainous landscape. The atmosphere was quite still and the plane moved calmly and steadily. Peter shut off the heat in the cabin, as the sun warmed sufficiently through the Plexiglas.

Geir looked at the clock and reckoned out his position according to their climb. He pulled the microphone nearer his mouth and called, "Bardufoss Control! This is Otter Three Two calling. Can you hear me? Over."

The great height gave a good connection and the answer came at once.

"Three Two from Bardufoss. Clearly and distinctly. Over."

"Bardufoss—Three Two. My position is 69 ° 18 ′ North, 21 ° 19 ′ East. I have just risen through the clouds from position eleven miles northwest of the Hellig Forest. Height 9,500 feet. Course 035 °. Calculated arrival at Kirkenes 12:15 P.M. Over."

"Understood from Bardufoss. Out."

Geir bent down over the map and ruled and reckoned for a time. "You can alter the course to 030," he said. "I hope the Weather Officer gave us an approximately correct wind. It's coming straight from the side and with the strength it has up here, it can drive us pretty far off our course."

"Yes, but the radio compass can put us right again as we approach the Varanger Fjord," said Peter.

Geir nodded.

They sat in silence, each thinking his own thoughts while the plane, flying steadily and evenly, ate up the miles. Geir shut his eyes, leaned back in his seat, and dozed a little. The monotonous cloud landscape below them was soporific.

Three-quarters of an hour later something happened.

Geir sat turning the radio compass trying to tune into Vadsö Radio when he suddenly started and sat bolt upright. The engine coughed and began to tick over unevenly. Both boys quickly scrutinized the instrument panel, and Geir took over the controls and pumped gas into the engine with the hand pump. It helped for a moment, but almost immediately things were going just as wrong again. Geir pushed the throttle right forward, but this only made things worse. The arrow on the altimeter flickered backwards and forwards. The drone of the engine rose and fell, and speed was diminishing quickly.

"What in the world can it be?" murmured Geir.

Peter jammed the earphones closer to his head.

"What did you say?" he shouted.

"What can be the matter?" repeated Geir more loudly.

"I don't know. Surely the carburetor can't be iced up in this dry, cold air?"

Geir shook his head.

"We're losing height," he said. "Hang on while I calculate our position. Keep the height as best you can."

He made a quick calculation and noted the time and the position on a slip of paper, which he tore off from the edge of the map. Peter tried desperately to keep the height, but the strength of the engine diminished more and more and their speed became critically low. He had to push the stick forward and glide in a slack curve down toward the clouds.

"This won't do. Send out an SOS," said Geir and handed Peter the piece of paper as he himself took over. "Say that we shall be obliged to jump for it if the engine doesn't recover itself. The ground below us rises to 2,500 feet and the clouds are almost certain to be right down over the peaks. We daren't take the chance of a forced landing."

Peter pressed the radio button. His hand was shaking a little.

"Mayday, mayday, mayday!" he shouted, trying to make his voice clear and distinct. "This is Otter Three Two, Three Two, Three Two. Over."

They listened anxiously. The plane was approaching the clouds. The radio crackled weakly, but no one answered.

Peter tried again.

"Mayday, mayday, mayday! Otter Three Two calling—Three Two, Three Two. Engine playing us up—reason unknown. Position 69 ° 36 ′ North, 23 ° 12 ′ East. We are flying 9,000 feet above thick cloud and losing height. Preparing to jump. Over."

The plane stuck its nose down into the clouds. It felt

pretty dismal seeing they were not descending of their own free will, but were sinking, sinking, into the gray mass in an almost unchangeable plane. The engine coughed and groaned worse than ever. Geir tried to maintain the flying speed and worked feverishly to keep the gliding angle as shallow as possible.

Suddenly both of them started. A weak, excited voice broke through the crackling of the radio. They sat immovable, straining every nerve to hear. Peter pressed the earphones close to his ears.

"Mayday, mayday, mayday. This is Alta Radio. Alta. Alta. Do you hear me? Three Two from Alta. Over."

Peter's voice was almost falsetto in his urgency. The words ran into each other.

"Alta from Three Two. Have you received my message? Over."

"Yes, I have your message. Repeat position for checking. Over!"

"O.K. Alta, position at 10:55, 69 ° 36 ′ North, 23 ° 12 ′ East. Over!"

"Position received. How goes it? Over!"

Geir pointed to the stick. "Increase the speed if you can," he said and then he himself pressed the radio button. He spoke as calmly as if he were giving a routine position report.

"Alta! We are down to 7,500 feet. The ground below us rises to 2,500. My co-pilot will jump when we pass 6,000. I shall circle his position until 4,500 when I shall make a forced landing if I catch a glimpse of the ground below us. Otherwise, I shall jump. Stand by. Out."

Geir turned to Peter and took over the controls again. He put his hand on Peter's shoulder and gave him an encouraging nod. "Clear the decks, Peter! Check your parachute straps and send your escape door overboard!"

An icy blast filled the cabin when Peter drew out the security pin from the door hinges and sent the door overboard.

The wind stormed round their ears and the cockpit was filled with the noise of the engine and the propeller.

Geir shouted loudly to be heard over the din.

"Jump, Peter! Best of luck!"

He forced a hasty smile and swung the plane toward the right in order to make the jump easier for Peter. He saw the soles of Peter's boots as he jumped out into the mist.

Geir let go of the stick with one hand and pressed the microphone close to his mouth. He turned his head a little to one side and put up his hand to shield his mouth from the blast from the open door.

"Alta, Three Two. My co-pilot has jumped. Height 5,800 feet—about 3,000 above the ground. I shall jump in about a minute. Thanks a lot, Alta. Out!"

He heard a little of the answer before he tore off the earphones and unloosed his escape door! "Best of luck! I shall . . ."

He quickly turned off the ignition, trimmed the plane for gliding in a northerly direction, unstrapped himself from the seat, and threw himself out.

Three — Alarm

Telegraph clerk John Berntsen at Alta hammered like a madman at the telegraph keys. He had sent an interim report to the Bodö coastal radio station while he was waiting for a telephonic connection with the Air Rescue Service in Bodö, and when the report had been sent, he leaned back in his chair and lit a cigarette with trembling hands. Behind him the stove crackled and spluttered, but outside the snow lay right up to the window sill and the clouds stood low and wet down the mountainsides. It was half dark, although it was the middle of the day. The contrast between the comfortless weather outside and the cozy room in which he himself was sitting made him feel the responsibility to be doubly heavy. Help must be obtained quickly.

He rang long distance and asked whether the connection would soon be in order.

"In a moment," said the operator. "I'm doing my best."

"All right, all right, and afterwards will you get me the head of police in Kautokeino. Try to get hold of him while I'm talking to Bodö."

He put down the receiver and stood up. He was too restless to sit still, and began to pace anxiously up and down the room.

At last the telephone rang.

"Hello, Bodö. Is that the Air Rescue Service?"

"Yes! Lieutenant Colonel Ruste here. I've just received your telegram. What happened?"

"They had engine trouble. They lost height and came down through a thick bank of clouds from 9,000 feet to about 2,000 above the ground. They could not take the chance to go lower and had to jump. The position and time were given in the telegram."

"Did it sound as if they were panicking?"

"Not in the least—their voices were entirely normal. The pilot circled for a moment or two after the co-pilot had jumped, and they have probably both come down quite close to each other. It should not be difficult to find them if the position given is correct, but if the weather there is no better than it is here, it's urgent—to put it mildly."

"What's it like with you?"

"Gray and cold. The height of the clouds is 5,000-6,000 feet and it's snowing off and on. It's not flying weather for anything but helicopters."

"No—I was afraid of that."

"What can I do?"

"Ask the Alta police to get together one or two bands of volunteers and members of the Red Cross. They should have equipment for spending the night. The chief of police will receive instruction about the search area a little later. One thing more—ask him to start a telephone foray within the area they might have flown over in his district in case someone may have heard them."

"Certainly! I have also put through a call to the head of police in Kautokeino. Shall I give him the same instructions?"

"Yes, please. And say that the helicopter will be coming sometime during the day."

"Is that all?"

"Yes—no, wait a moment. We'll send a 'Norseman' to Kirkenes to deal with that ambulance job, and on his way the pilot will try to estimate the rate of the wind at 9,000 feet so that we can check on the rate given in the weather warning. Keep in touch with him and let me know if he has anything of importance to report. 'Morning."

" 'Morning!"

Ruste got up and walked straight across the floor to a large wall map where an Air Traffic Controller and the Weather Officer were standing talking to each other in low voices. The Air Traffic Controller had drawn a circle round the area on the map with a red pencil.

"This is the search area," he said. "I have allowed for a possible 12 per cent navigational error in the distance they flew after their last known position. It will be strange if they are not within this circle."

Ruste lit a cigarette, and it hung from the corner of his mouth while he studied the map with half-closed eyes.

"Well!" he said at last. "Analyze the district and divide it up between one helicopter—pity that we've only one available at the moment—and three patrols. But first of all we must collect the rescue personnel. Ask the head of police to send a man, and telephone the Rescue Officer and the representative of the Red Cross. Has the commanding officer at the station been informed?"

The Air Traffic Controller nodded. "Control's done that. All the branches of the Air Rescue Service are standing by. Bardufoss and Skattöra have been warned, and Bardufoss have started up a telephone foray so as to chart the route to Skibotten."

Ruste nodded. He turned away from the map and went back to his desk.

"Is there any chance of it clearing?" he asked the Weather Officer.

"No." The Weather Officer shook his head. "I don't think so. This sort of weather can go on for weeks on end."

Ruste sat down at his desk, supporting his chin in his hand. He did not reply. A little later he lifted the receiver.

"Helicopters," he said.

He heard a click, and then such a loud, strong voice answered that he instinctively held the receiver a short distance away from his ear.

"Helicopter Officer in charge," said the voice. "Lieutenant Rowan!"

"Listen, Rowan—this is Ruste. You've heard about the Otter, I suppose!"

"Yes!"

"Well, take off for Bardufoss at once and arrange to go on to Kautokeino today. You'll receive more precise instructions over the radio or when you land at Bardufoss."

"Right. I'll be in the air within five minutes. What was it that—? No, that can wait. I'll start at once. 'Morning!"

" 'Morning!"

A major from Traffic Control came in as Ruste put down the receiver. He was the Rescue Officer.

"Anything fresh?" he asked and hung his coat over the back of a chair.

"Not yet," said Ruste. "But we've started up all the routine inquiries in order to chart the route. As a matter of fact, we know just about where the accident happened. I don't think it will be difficult to find them."

"It would have been as easy as winking if we could have sent planes," said the Air Traffic Controller. "But it will be difficult even for the helicopter to keep below the clouds in this weather."

"Yes—it's always like that when anything happens," said Ruste. "Crashes and bad weather always seem to go together."

The two other members of the Air Rescue Service arrived together by car from Bodö. Ruste arranged chairs and tables in a half circle in front of the wall map, left the telephone to the Air Traffic Controller, and gave an account of how the accident had happened and what had already been done by the Air Rescue Service. Then they discussed the matter in all its aspects and came to the conclusion that not much more could be done at present. The search area was approved, and they reckoned that both the patrols and the helicopter would be in action from the following morning. The helicopter was to keep in touch with the patrols so that they could report alterations in the search area if necessary. Furthermore, an announcement on the radio would urge anyone who had seen or heard the plane to get in touch with the nearest head of police.

"Everything points to the probability that this rescue operation will be very simple," said Ruste. "If the position they gave us was anything like accurate, I think we ought to have them home safe and sound tomorrow."

While this was going on, Svein was flying northward and had reached a point a few miles past Tjeldsund when he was called up by Harstad Radio. He made haste to answer.

"Harstad from Helicopter One Four. Over."

"One Four from Harstad. Bodö says that you are to fill up in Bardufoss as soon as possible and go straight on to Kautokeino. You will have a passenger, a policeman from Tromsö who is going to help in the search. The weather report will be brought to the helicopter. The search will begin at dawn tomorrow. You'll be given further orders through the head of police in Kautokeino. Over."

"O.K. Harstad. What's the weather like at Bardufoss? Over."

"Good! Clouds 7,000-8,000 feet. It's not snowing. Over."

"Thanks! One Four out."

Svein had never before been so intensely aware of the slow pace of the helicopter. Impatience gnawed like a rat at his innards. The wind was almost directly against him, and his speed was less than sixty miles an hour, although he forced the engine far beyond its usual capacity.

The technician who sat beside him measured the distance to Kautokeino on the map and shook his head doubtfully.

"It will be difficult to get there before dark," he announced.

"We'll manage it," said Svein. "We shall have the wind from the side when we fly from Bardufoss."

Thoughtfully he gazed at the wild, white-clad mountain range along the coast. The grayish-black covering of clouds hid the peaks like a dirty blanket stretching right out to the horizon. The rotor outlined a clear circle shining weakly against the sky.

"Tomorrow—" he thought. "After an icy cold night—"

Four — Where Is Peter?

The moment Geir threw himself out of the plane he had an almost irresistible urge to pull the release cord of the parachute. When he had sat at the controls inside the plane a moment ago, he had had a good idea of his height above the ground, for both the controls and the map had shown him this and he had depended on them. But now as he rushed downward through the white impenetrable mist, the eeriness of it all sent cold shivers down his spine. What if he had mistaken the height! He felt as if at any moment the earth might come storming up toward him, or that a rock, like some black clenched fist, might suddenly appear through the mist and smash him to bits.

Involuntarily he took a firm hold of the release cord—but he did not pull it. Many a time he had imagined himself in this situation. Many a time he had reckoned out the number of seconds he must allow to pass before he could be sure he was clear of the plane. Now his brain and muscles reacted mechanically against the feeling of panic that almost mastered him because the mist was blinding him.

When at last he pulled the cord, he was not sure how long it was since he had jumped, but he felt as if he had fallen many hundreds of feet. The parachute flapped behind him, and time stood still for a moment. Then came the jerk—and a loud bang just above him. He must have been falling head foremost, for he felt as if somebody had taken a powerful grip on his shoulders and jerked him up into a perpendicular position. Everything went black. Then the blackness turned into a confused glimmering of dancing blue and red dots that floated slowly away.

His body rocked violently underneath the cords, and now and then he had the impression that the parachute lay below him. The feeling of what was either above him or below was far from clear. The air stream changed its direction as he swung, and he had no fixed point for his eyes except the parachute umbrella itself.

By degrees he was able to steady the worst of the rocking by pulling systematically at some of the cords above him. That made him feel more secure, but he still had the strange feeling that the ground might suddenly and unexpectedly rush up toward him out of the mist, and he bent his knees and braced his muscles so that he might be ready to receive it.

Then—almost as if by magic—he was in clear air. It was like coming up to the top after swimming under water. He felt that not until now had he been able to breathe freely.

The snow-covered ground lay a few hundred feet below him, an undulating plain with low hillocks and ridges darkened here and there by scattered, low-growing forest.

Geir picked out a fairly level piece of ground and tried to steer toward it by pulling the edge of the parachute down to one side, thus using it like a sail and trimming it to the right direction for the wind. He was successful. He landed right in the middle of a deep snowdrift into which he sank to above his knees. But the next moment the parachute had pulled him up out of the drift and had thrown him over onto his back. The parachute stood out like a huge sail above him, dragging him along at such a pace through the snow that it rose in a whirl around him. His first impulse was to free himself from the parachute, but happily he caught himself in time. It was far too valuable a thing to lose. With tightly closed eyes, he struggled blindly with the cords above him and finally caught hold of a couple and hauled them in. The parachute flapped and his speed diminished as he wound in the cords yard by yard. Finally a gust of wind caught hold of the top of the parachute and threw it onto the ground. It still heaved about in the wind and threw him down every time he tried to get up, but by continuing to pull at the strings, he was, in the end, able to crush the parachute down under him and roll it up into a bundle.

Then he trampled down the snow in a little circle round him, wriggled himself out of his pigskin jacket and shook it, poked out the snow from his neck and wrists, and brushed it off his trousers. Then he straightened his back and began to take stock of his surroundings.

He was standing in the midst of rugged, undulating country that rose and fell in long lines and alternated between level stretches of ground and slopes, low mountain ridges and little hills.

Here and there rocks or large boulders showed up black against the snow, and on the mountainsides, which naturally faced south, grew stunted birches and willows. He had a glimpse of mountains far away rising high into the air.

The wind was icy cold. Low, tattered clouds chased each other across the sky, and showers of fine snow were blown about above the high snowdrifts with a whistling sound.

Geir stared anxiously in the direction where he thought the north should be. With any luck he might get a glimpse of the plane before it actually crashed. Possibly it might survive its landing if it had been trimmed rightly and if it landed on its skis on level ground. But he could neither hear nor see anything, and after a minute or two he gave up. He would hunt for it later, he decided; just at this moment it was more important to find Peter.

But where could he be? The landscape around Geir was entirely empty and lifeless in all directions as far as he could see. They must have drifted pretty far from each other. Perhaps it would be best to wait a little. It was not improbable that Peter had seen him when he broke through the clouds and was even now on his way toward him.

Geir cupped his hands in front of his mouth like a trumpet and shouted, "Ahoy! Ahoy!"

He then turned his back to the wind, put his hands behind his ears, and tried to catch any sound that differed from the howling of the wind, but whichever way he turned and twisted, his ears were filled only with the noise of the wind, rising and falling, and the continuous flapping of his own clothes and of the bundled parachute beside him. After all, they would have to be pretty close to each other to be able to make contact by shouting.

Again he collected the air into his lungs and shouted with might and main.

"A-hoy-y! Peter, a-hoy-y!" But not a sound answered him.

Geir shuddered. He had not reckoned on this.

He made a quick calculation. Peter had hung in his parachute for about a minute and a half longer than he had. At the very worst the wind could not have carried him more than just over a mile away to the southeast. In that direction the ground was rugged and difficult to survey, and it would be hard to walk over in the deep snow, especially as they did not have their bearings straight toward each other, so to speak.

Well—at any rate he would have the wind behind him.

He unbuckled the rubber dinghy that was fastened to the parachute harness and opened the little valve of the oxygen flask. The dinghy filled up with a hissing sound, unrolling itself at once. The wind took hold of it immediately, and it was only at the last moment that he was able to throw himself over it as it turned a somersault and was about to be blown away from him. Then he had to trample down more snow in order to make a sheltered place for the dinghy too. This did not look promising. He had meant to use the dinghy as a sledge, but if it was going to behave like a balloon, he had better deflate it again and try to carry both it and the parachute.

For safety's sake he stood with one foot in the dinghy while he brushed the snow off the parachute and rolled it up into a tight bundle. He fastened the parachute and his life belt into the bottom of the dinghy with one of the parachute cords, thus turning it into a sledge, and finally harnessed himself to the front of it with two cords running from the sledge to his parachute harness, which he had put on again. After another searching look around him, he started to walk in the deep snow.

He sank down to his knees and after a few moments was panting like a whale. He stopped to look back. He had not covered many yards.

"If only I had skis," he thought, "or snowshoes."

He wriggled out of his leather jacket and put it in the sledge also. He must not allow himself to sweat. Damp clothes in this wind and cold would not only be uncomfortable but downright dangerous.

After a few hundred yards he was so exhausted that he had to lift his legs out of the deep snow with his hands. He progressed at a snail's pace. In the deepest snowdrifts and in packed snow he had to creep on all fours, and suddenly he would be knocked over by the dinghy, which would be thrown right around when the wind caught it.

He tried to shout now and again but got no answer—nor did he expect it, for after all he was not much nearer than when he started.

Nearer—? Suddenly the blood rushed to his cheeks as the thought went through his brain like a streak of lightning. Could he be walking in the wrong direction? In his hurry he had reckoned that Peter had drifted furthest because he had jumped from a greater height and had hung in his parachute for a moment or two longer, but after all, that was not really conclusive.

Geir stood still with a frown between his eyes and a

puzzled expression about his mouth. He was thinking so hard that he practically heard his brain creak.

He himself who had been in the air longest must have drifted furthest. It made no difference whether he had been circling in the plane or been dangling in the parachute. On the contrary—the wind was stronger at the greater height and must therefore have driven him more quickly while he was circling. The two minutes that he had probably been in the air after Peter had landed might mean, perhaps, almost three miles—and in absolutely the opposite direction!

Discouraged, he turned round against the wind and looked at the tracks he had just made. It seemed so hopeless to begin trudging the same way back.

Then an idea struck him that cheered him up a little. He remembered that his dinghy bag, that is, the bag in which the dinghy had been packed, was stiffened with a veneered plywood square. Surely it could be used as a snowshoe; at any rate it would help him along to the nearest bed of willows where he would be able to find material for better snowshoes.

He pulled the dinghy eagerly toward him and found the bag with the plywood square just underneath the parachute. He had a good knife in a special pocket in his uniform, and he used it to make two rows of three holes each along the middle of the square, and through these he threaded parachute cords to act as shoestrings.

It worked. He fastened the snowshoe onto his right boot and took a step to test it. It actually held him up, and by taking first a long, sliding step and then a short one, he limped along much more quickly than before. He followed his old track for part of the way and then changed his direction toward a little mound where he saw some bushes sticking up out of the snow.

It took him a quarter of an hour to get there.

The branches reaching up to the top of the snow were too thin for his purpose, but he dug down along one of the stems and found that it grew thicker and thicker, until it divided itself into two, forming another branch. He knelt and cut it off just below the fork. This would serve his purpose well. He bent the two branches toward each other and tied them together with a parachute cord, thus forming an oval. Then he braided the cord longways and crossways, making a net reaching from side to side of the bent branches. It took him half an hour to finish this snowshoe, and he could not allow himself time to make another.

Now he must hurry on. Not that the snowshoes were masterpieces. The braided one sank too deeply into the snow because it was rather too small, and the wooden square, being veneered, was slippery and slid down into the snow whenever he trod sideways on it. But he was content. The time that he had taken was not ill spent, and he reckoned that he would now soon be in touch with Peter.

He reached the top of a low hill. Behind it the ground slanted downwards some hundred yards to a level piece of ground, which he reckoned must be a lake. On a slope leading to a long range of hills on the opposite side of the lake—to the north to judge from the direction of the wind —grew a whole luxurious wood of birch trees. It looked so calm and lovely there. The wind did not whirl the snow about as it did everywhere else.

"That may be a good camping place," was Geir's first impression. "We shall find both building material and firewood there."

But there was no sign of Peter. He called and shouted again and again, looked around in all directions, shouted and listened. But not even an echo answered him. The wind howled so loudly in his ears that he could scarcely hear his own shouts.

Should he use one of the signal rockets? Could he afford that? He did not remember exactly how many there were in each dinghy; he thought four—possibly six. But they might mean life or death later on when the planes came to search for them. Probably it would be best to wait a little, at any rate until he reached the top of that hill.

A little farther up the slope, away from the lake, he found that it was much more sheltered. He needed a rest and stood for a moment leaning against a boulder, which lay some fifty to sixty yards from the lake.

"This is where we must build our hut," he thought. "We can dig ourselves in under the shelter of this boulder and make a sort of tent of birch branches and parachute silk."

The thought was tempting. To sit in a dry hut eating his emergency rations and then smoking a pipe was a dream—a temptation he was obliged to resist.

He decided to leave the dinghy here beside the boulder, but he remembered to take two signal rockets with him.

It was tricky walking along the grassy mountainside.

Willows and other bushes stuck up through the snow everywhere, and stunted birches with long beards stood huddled together. He noticed with satisfaction that some of them were as much as two or three yards above the snow level. Here and there he found dead trees with dry, barkless trunks. They would make good firewood, he thought.

Yes—here was the place for their camp. He became quite certain of this when, on nearing the top, he came across the trail of some birds that went in and out among the bushes.

"Ptarmigan," he thought to himself, and suddenly felt hungry.

In front of him lay a long, undulating stretch of almost unbroken white, which reached as far as another range of hills several miles away.

Geir stood there for a long time, filled with wonder, his eyes searching for some sign of life. Peter must be somewhere on this plain. But where? There was nothing at all to be seen—not a smudge or blur of any kind, not a movement, to give him even a little hope. If Peter were on his way toward him, he could not remain hidden for long behind the little mounds dotted about this plain, and if he were resting, surely he would not be so stupid as to sit hidden away in some little dell. But where in the world could he be then? Had he gone in an entirely wrong direction, reckoned wrongly—as he himself had before he had really worked out the situation? In that case Peter might well be behind the ridge on the other side of the plain, and that meant that nothing more could be done today. If he were to get there, he must first go and fetch the dinghy, and it might perhaps be dark before he got there. Besides, he did not really believe in that theory. Peter could scarcely have walked so far. It was more likely he had chosen the way south of the lake in order to circle the ridge on which he himself now stood. From Peter's side no doubt that way looked easier, and it would not lead him very far out of the direction of the wind. But Geir could not rid himself of the thought that Peter must have been very short-sighted, not to say stupid, if he had not tried to get up onto some high ground to get a good view all around.

Geir began to feel a nagging anxiety. Something must have happened. Perhaps Peter was injured. Perhaps—worse than that.

He looked at his watch and gave a start. How quickly the time had gone. Two hours had already passed since he reached the ground. He must hurry now.

He quickly made a plan. If he followed the ridge toward the south, he could look out for tracks and then swing out across the plain lower down if he did not find anything.

In order to avoid the small ups and downs on the top of the ridge, he followed it a little lower down walking along the lower slope. The snow had been blown in drifts into which he sank deeply now and again. He felt the perspiration running down his back, and he stopped to open his jacket and shirt at the neck. Just by chance he touched his breast pocket into which he had put the signal rockets.

"Idiot," he said to himself aloud.

If there was a time when it was necessary to use signal rockets, surely it was now. If Peter lay injured in the snow in this cold, minutes might be decisive.

Feverishly he unpacked one of the rockets and read through the instructions quickly. Then he held it high above his head and pulled the rip-cord. A red flare curved into the sky and a few seconds later another.

His heart beat so violently that he could hear it. He blinked in the cold wind as his eyes searched the white expanse. A minute passed, perhaps more.

Then a red light flickered across the snow scarcely a mile away. It rose over the crest of a hill and then disappeared.

Five — In Camp

Geir was sweaty and out of breath when he finally reached the crest of the hill and saw Peter lying a little below him down the slope.

"Hey! Peter," he shouted, feeling relieved and frightened. "Are you hurt?"

Peter did not answer until Geir stopped beside him. Then a faint smile flitted across his pale face and he said, "Yes, I'm afraid I am. I slipped on a stone as I landed and I think I've broken my leg."

The snow was uneven and was bunched into little heaps around Peter. It looked as if it were covering a rock-strewn slope. He had rolled himself up in the parachute like a cocoon and was leaning against the dinghy with his head sticking out of the silk.

"Are you cold?" asked Geir.

"A little," said Peter. His lips were trembling and looked suspiciously blue.

"I've rolled most of the stuff around my legs so that my broken leg wouldn't get frostbitten. It took a long time and hurt like the devil, but I think I've managed to keep it more or less warm. I still have feeling in my toes."

"Thank God!" said Geir.

He looked around briskly hoping to find something that he could use as a splint, but the branches of the small bushes around them were too short and crooked to be of use. On the other hand, the paddle oars from the dinghy might be useful, for with them as main supports and small twigs in between, he could, he thought, splint up Peter's leg fairly effectively for the time being.

"Are you very wet?" Geir asked.

"Yes, but only my behind. I couldn't get the parachute under me properly. My backside's melting the snow under me."

Geir did not answer but set about the work to be done. While he tore long strips of the parachute material and found the paddle oars, he told Peter about the camping place he had found and they decided to get there if Geir was able to pull the dinghy through the snow with Peter in it. They could not settle down on the open plain for the night. They must find shelter from the wind, and they also needed wood with which to make a fire to keep themselves warm if they were to survive the night.

After he had been to all the nearest bushes and had found some branches that were not too crooked to use, Geir had all he needed for splinting Peter's leg. He began by folding the parachute to one side.

"Shout if it hurts," he said. "Don't mind me!"

Peter shook his head. "I'll shout like a maniac if I feel anything," he said, but his voice was strained and his facial muscles were so taut that he had turned quite white.

Geir's hands trembled, partly from nervousness and partly because he had begun to shiver with cold, but he had no time to think of himself. He loosened the laces of Peter's boot, inserted the knife in the boot, and slit it open right out to the toe. Then he was able to get it off quite easily. Happily Peter's sock was dry and he left it on for the moment. He cut Peter's trousers to above the knee and carefully felt the break. The leg was very swollen and lay a little crookedly. But in spite of everything, he felt relieved. It was not as bad as he had feared.

Peter looked at him questioningly but without saying anything, and Geir nodded encouragement.

"It looks all right," he said. "Now I am going to work quickly. You must clench your teeth while I straighten out your leg. It is so nearly straight that it would be a pity to let it knit crookedly, as I think we must not reckon on being found for a few days at any rate. Besides, as it is now, it is neither quite straight nor quite crooked, and I don't believe I could get a splint to hold it in that position. What do you think yourself?"

"The same as you," said Peter. "Let's get it over with. Just at the moment it is so damned painful that a little more or less won't make much difference."

Mostly to overcome his own uncertainty Geir went on talking.

"The bones are so nearly in place," he said, "that no more is needed than a little stretch as far as I can see. You can shout as loud as you like, if it helps. There—that ought to be all right. Now it's done."

Peter groaned weakly. He closed his eyes and pressed his lips together. His hands fumbled in the parachute silk as if he were trying to find something to hold on to.

Geir did not look at him. He pulled off Peter's sock and carefully examined his foot. It was cold, but the circulation seemed all right. Happily none of the toes were white. Frostbite would have been far more dangerous than the break.

He pulled on Peter's sock again carefully and wound strips of parachute silk around the leg from above the knee right down to the foot. Then he laid the paddle oars and the branches along the leg as splints and bound them tightly around with silk and parachute cord.

"How's that feel?" he asked as he stood up.

"Too good to be true," said Peter.

"You've been lucky. You've no frostbite—unless your backside has it."

"I shouldn't be surprised. I've never been so wet in the pants since I was a year old."

"I don't suppose you've had diapers since then either," said Geir, "but now you're going to have them."

He cut two large squares of parachute silk and doubled them together, and then, catching hold of Peter under his arms, he pulled him up onto his legs and supported him. Together, and with great struggles, they turned down the wet trousers as far as the knees and filled them with the silk squares. Then they pulled his trousers up again.

"I didn't think you'd find me," said Peter a little later when he lay in the dinghy with the parachute packed around him and tightly fastened down with cross cords.

"I was nearly giving up. I had used up half of my six rockets."

Geir had seen the empty cases lying in the snow.

"They didn't go high enough," he said. "I couldn't see them on the other side of the ridge. I landed more than two miles to the south of you."

"Had you expected that?"

"Well—just about, but I thought you were probably walking in a wrong direction, either going away from me or else round me."

Geir fastened two cords onto the dinghy and bound them round his waist; then he leaned forward, dug his heels into the snow, and pulled with all his might. With a jerk the sledge began to move. It was going to work. They were on their way.

Geir was shivering with cold. Not until now had he realized that his underclothes were wet through from perspiration. It was good to be moving about again, and at first, he wasted his strength. But both his snowshoes and the dinghy sank deeply into the snow, and it was not long before the sweat began to run down his forehead again. He was obliged to stop and rest almost cvcry minute, and he pulled off one garment after another for fear of getting too hot. His leather jacket, his cap, his scarf, and his gloves were stowed away under the parachute with Peter.

It was past two o'clock. It would be dark in less than three hours. The rest of the day was going to be a race with time.

Three-quarters of an hour later Geir dragged himself panting and exhausted over the last few yards and came to a halt beside the big boulder. He lay down in his own dinghy and shut his eyes. His legs were as heavy as lead. He felt as if he would never be able to get up again.

Peter looked at him anxiously. "You'll burst yourself!" he said. He could think of nothing else to say.

"Oh, shut up." Geir pulled himself together. He had no reason to be cross. The job had to be done and what had happened was nobody's fault. He might have been the unlucky one as easily as Peter.

"I'll be all right," he said in a lighter tone of voice. He scrambled to his legs and almost fell when he began moving without anything to drag. His underclothes were clammy and disgusting. He hummed a little tune; then he pulled off garment after garment down to his waist and stood naked in the cold air.

Peter shuddered but said nothing. Geir rubbed himself down with a piece of the parachute silk, shook out his underclothes, and then pulled them on again. It helped. When he had put on all his clothes again, he felt warm and a great deal more cheerful. He dragged Peter to the sheltered side of the boulder.

"You'll have to settle down here for an hour or two," he said. "I must use every moment of daylight."

When a little later he stood in the wood, choosing a small and suitable birch tree, he spared a grateful thought to whoever had arranged that a large sharp knife should be included in their emergency kit. The knife cut its way through the fairly thick trunks of the small trees in a couple of minutes. He picked out the straightest trees he could find, three or four yards high, and collected them in a heap at the edge of the wood. It was enough to go on with. They were unusually lucky. In many places on the moor there were only low, crooked, windblown trees that would have been no good for anything.

He managed to overcome his fatigue after the march and worked quickly and effectively. At the side of the heap of straight trunks, he collected a smaller heap of wood, mostly dry branches that looked as if they would burn well.

Peter watched him as he began dragging the wood to the camping ground.

"Can I help you with anything?" he asked.

"Tja, you can come up and fetch the rest," said Geir ironically.

"I can strip off the twigs for you."

"No, you'll only cover yourself with snow and get wet."

Geir brushed the snow from the boulder and cleared a square in front of it, using the plywood square from Peter's dinghy bag to dig with. Then he dragged Peter to the side, turning him sideways so that he had to turn his head almost out of its socket if he wanted to see what Geir was doing. It seemed as if Geir wished to make quite sure that Peter could not take any part in the work. Peter felt a little hurt, but he said nothing.

The work progressed. When the space was cleared, Geir stripped the straightest of the trees and drove them down into the snow along the side of the clearing. Then he laid horizontal trunks as a roof from the boulder to the upright trunks and bound them together at the top of the uprights with the parachute cords. He tied thinner trunks slantingly across the walls and crosswise on the roof. The hut was about the height of a man from the floor to the roof and almost six feet square.

Peter remained silent, but he began to wonder how long Geir actually thought they would remain here. He himself would not have considered it necessary to put so much work into a hut for one night.

Geir moved away a couple of steps and looked at his work.

"That will hold for today," he said. "It will soon be dark, and I would rather do a little more on it tomorrow. I'll use half my parachute as insulation, and it will cover threefold I think. With a little snow on the roof and on the walls, it will be warm enough, don't you think?"

"Quite a villa," said Peter.

"Do you want a job?"

"Rather!"

"Break up these twigs quite small and throw them on the floor."

"O.K., pull me over there."

They worked together in silence for a time. Geir put his twigs on the roof and Peter threw his on the floor. Then Geir trampled down the snow in a half circle in front of the entrance, cut up some of the branches into lengths of about half a yard, placing them beside each other a few steps away from the door.

Peter imagined that this was to be the base of a camp-fire.

"Won't they all burn up?" he asked.

"Of course, but much slower than the wood that does

not come in contact with the snow," said Geir. "Can you peel off some bark for me?"

He picked out the driest branches he could find and piled them carefully in a heap on the top of the prepared branches he had already arranged there. Peter handed him the bark. Geir shoved it in underneath with a piece of paper—an old letter he had found in his breast pocket. He kept the envelope till later.

They watched the early flames eagerly. The paper burned quickly and the tongues of flame came licking up between the twigs. The bark caught fire after a while. It rolled up and crackled. Gradually the fire increased in strength, and one branch after another caught fire. A tongue of flame shot up here and there in the heap of branches, but as soon as the bark had burned out, the fire quickly died down.

"Do you know any magic words for making fires burn?" whispered Peter.

"More bark," said Geir.

He got hold of a few pieces of bark and held them close to a small flame until they caught fire.

"More! More! Pull off all the bark you can reach," he said.

Peter worked feverishly, and Geir pushed the bark under the wood as Peter handed it to him. It began to hold. More and more branches caught fire. The small flames joined the larger ones, and a spiral of smoke whirled up into the cold air.

It was growing dark, but neither of them had noticed it before. The fire now began to flame up in earnest, and they saw that the landscape around them was beginning to fade out, and their world quickly diminished into a little circle round the flickering light from the fire.

They sat for a long time staring into the flames, Peter in his dinghy and Geir on his heels in front of the fire.

An almost solemn feeling came over them. Fear of the cold and perhaps also of the darkness had subconsciously been the driving force in them both ever since they had landed on the snow. Now these fears were banished and with it came relief that the worst danger seemed almost over. Perhaps the old cave-dwellers felt the same when they collected round their campfires while darkness closed in on them from every side.

Peter finally broke the silence.

"I've read that man made his greatest advances when he had obtained dominion over fire. I suppose it was then that the transition from animals to human beings actually took place."

"Possibly," said Geir drily. He got up quickly and added, "Anyhow, I'm glad that the Air Rescue Service had the sense to put matches in our emergency packs. I should not like to have to make fire by rubbing stones together as in olden days."

He threw some bigger branches onto the flames and dragged Peter a little farther away from the heat. In the light of the fire he began to fasten up the parachute silk round the walls.

Finally they were able to settle down. The two dinghies had plenty of room beside each other on a thick dry layer of branches, and the fire outside sent a half light and a flood of warmth in through the door opening.

Geir laid his life jacket and the back cushion from the parachute harness at the bottom of his dinghy and made a bed with the remains of the parachute silk. He felt that the last shreds of strength and his will to keep going were on the point of deserting him. His stomach cried out for food, and he remembered that he had not tasted either food or drink since he had eaten at Bardufoss. So now, at last, it was time to examine what they had in their emergency rations. He had not thought of this until now when fatigue was about to overcome him. He was altogether tired out. He shut his eyes and lay with his head on his elbows for a time. Then he rolled over onto his back with a sigh and threw a piece of the parachute silk over him.

"I ought to see what food we have," he said in a tired, die-away voice. "I'll just rest a little first."

"It's a wonder that you haven't fallen headlong before this," said Peter. "Lie down and have a sleep; we ought to save our food as long as possible anyhow."

Geir heard Peter's voice as if it came from very far away. The warmth from the fire tickled his face comfortably, his aching muscles relaxed, his breathing became even and calm, and he fell into a heavy sleep.

Peter lay on his back looking at the flickering light of the fire that came in through the door. It had been a strange day—from the moment when he, almost in the middle of the night, had sat on the edge of his bed hoping to be allowed to join in the trip, up to this moment when he was lying in a primitive hut in wild country, far away from inhabited regions. In his thoughts he could see Geir again in various situations, speaking little, often quite silent, but friendly in his way and always calm and sure of himself. The idea that had occurred to him that morning at the breakfast table—that it was a very long way to Geir's confidence—was probably correct. A day like today ought to have brought them closer together, but it did not seem to have done so.

The crackling of the fire and the soft warmth that slowly spread through the hut as the stone behind it grew warm, made Peter sleepy too. His eyes slowly closed.

Outside the fire sent up a rain of sparks over the snow; then the flames died calmly and evenly away, and after some hours there was only a tiny line of smoke rising from a black heap of ashes.

Six — A Dangerous Expedition

Geir woke when the first streak of dawn appeared on the horizon. He was shivering a little and felt exceedingly stiff, but thoroughly rested after his sleep. Before he went out, he pulled off some of the bark from the nearest tree trunks in the wall of the hut and lit a blazing fire with the few remaining branches in his pile of wood. Then he fastened on his snowshoes and went off to gather more firewood. When he came back, Peter was awake and it was fully light.

" 'Morning!" said Geir. "How are you feeling?"

"Fine," said Peter.

"What do you mean? Do you feel really fine or only as far as possible in the circumstances?"

"Yes, better than I had expected. My leg is grumbling and throbbing a bit, but I feel in good form on the whole. What about you?"

"Only starving."

Peter raised himself on his elbow and nodded, smiling. "I believe you," he said. "My innards are shrieking for food. I don't think you ought to do any work until you have got something inside you."

"The firewood was practically finished," said Geir, and crept back into the hut. "I have a lot to do. The weather looks threatening and the wind is freshening. I should not be surprised if we had snow."

He opened one of their boxes of emergency rations and spread out the contents.

"You can decide the menu," he said. "Chocolate, fruit bar, caramels, or boiled sweets?"

"I could eat the lot," said Peter, "but I suppose we will have to make do with chocolate."

"And soup," said Geir, "hot soup, the best we have."

The rations were packed in aluminum boxes. Geir emptied the other box too and filled them both with snow. Then he put them on the hot embers at the edge of the fire, filling them up with more snow as it melted so that they were almost full of water. Finally he put bouillon cubes into the boiling water and stirred them with pieces of stick. It seemed to take an endless time for the water to boil—longer than they had imagined possible. At any rate, that is how they felt.

But it was worth waiting for. When they began to gulp down the scalding liquid, neither of them paused until their boxes were empty. It seemed a drink for the gods.

Afterwards they munched chocolate slowly and thoughtfully. The heat from the fire had already warmed up the hut enough for them to take off their leather coats. Geir examined his pipe thoughtfully. It was half full. He had left his tobacco in the plane. He looked so unhappy that Peter was forced to smile, but he grew serious immediately.

"You'll have six cigarettes," he said, "three in each emergency packet. It's a good thing I don't smoke, so that I'm not altogether useless."

Geir shrugged his shoulders. "Cigarettes are just to ginger up your appetite," he said. "They aren't really smoking." Then he pulled himself together and looked at Peter apologetically. "Well, they come in useful when one has nothing else," he added.

An uncertain smile flickered across Peter's face.

"You would have got on much better without a second pilot on this particular trip," he said in a low voice.

"Nonsense," said Geir.

"I have only been a bother—and I shouldn't have been worth much if you hadn't—"

"Don't talk rubbish!" Geir interrupted. He sounded angry. "Stop all that nonsense." But Peter would not give in.

"But for me you could have walked to Alta," he added reluctantly. "It isn't so very far, and you could have got there in a couple of days."

"What damned idiotic ideas you have," said Geir with a laugh. "Let's get this straight once and for all. To begin with, there always have to be two to fly the Otter, and you did it quite as well as anybody else who has flown with me. Secondly, you landed in a more unfortunate place than I did, but it might just as easily have been the other way around. Thirdly, it would never have occurred to me to be so mad as to set out across the moor with neither a map nor a weather forecast in the middle of winter. I would have stayed where I thought they would search for me, and I would have done that whether I was alone or not. As a matter of fact, I am only too glad that I'm not alone."

Geir got up abruptly and crawled out through the door without waiting for an answer. He turned his broad back demonstratively toward Peter while he broke off a twig and pushed it down his pipe. There was an angry gurgling in the bowl for a moment until he drew the smoke more slowly, when a mild and satisfied expression spread over his face. He looked thoughtfully around and began to plan out the day's work.

During the next few hours he dragged one load of birch trees after another to the hut and pulled the branches off the trunks outside. He cut off some of the straightest tops and used them for new splints for Peter's leg. These splints were straight and stiff and reached from his hip to the sole of his foot, and Peter insisted that he could walk with them.

Later in the day Geir took the parachute off the hut. He added some more tree trunks and several crossbands in the walls. He put crossbeams on the roof between the old ones and doubled the layer of twigs. Then he put the parachute back and cut out square blocks of the hardest snow and piled them up against the walls.

"Isn't there anything I can do?" asked Peter, feeling a little out of things.

Geir straightened his back and allowed himself a little rest. He lit one of the cigarettes from the emergency packet and sat down on his heels beside the fire looking out across the lake.

"Can you knot fishing lines?"

"I'm an expert in that sort of thing," said Peter. "There is a picture of a net on the outside of the box in which my favorite sardines are packed, or perhaps it's only a sweep net!"

Geir stubbed out his cigarette after only a couple of puffs and began to work again.

"Where is your home?" he asked.

"The East Coast," announced Peter. "Can't you hear it by my accent?"

"No."

"What about you? From Fredrikstad?"

"Sarpsborg."

"Well, now we know that. Otherwise we don't know much about each other."

"No."

"What shall I make the fishing tackle of? The parachute cords?"

"There's nothing else. First of all you can braid them into single lines. We need these for snares, too. I saw traces of a ptarmigan up on the mountainside yesterday."

Peter raised himself up on his elbow and leaned forward so as to see Geir through the door.

"You're reckoning that we shall be here some time."

"Of course. Surely you yourself don't feel certain that we shall be found today?"

"N-no, but they know where we are."

"In a way, yes, but we may be miles away from the position we gave them, and if that was wrong—where will they look? What mistake will they reckon we've made? It will be pure luck if they come here straight away. Again, we don't know how long the weather will hold. If it begins to snow, they will have to postpone looking for us."

Peter nodded gravely. "I hope my leg will knit before the spring," he said. "Then there will be a chance of finding our way to Alta or Kautokeino, or we'll be able to contact some hunter or other."

By midday Geir had put the finishing touches to the hut. Both the walls and the roof were enclosed with almost two feet of snow, only a small air hole being left at the top of the roof on the lee side. The door could be shut with parachute cord. The layer of branches on the floor almost hid the bare ground, and outside Geir had trampled down a large square. On the windy side the hut was protected by a snow wall about six feet high, and in one corner lay a huge heap of wood—enough for the following day and night, and perhaps more.

Meanwhile, Peter had braided up some of the nylon string, and Geir did not give himself time to rest on his oars. He immediately went out to lay the snares. He planted low fences of fresh twigs in the snow in among the low bushes, leaving small openings some feet apart, which he closed with snares. In one or two places he tried double fences in the form of an arrow, fastening the snares in the sharp end. He hoped that when the ptarmigans came to browse the buds off the twigs, they would be led toward the snare and push their heads into the noose when they entered the opening.

"It's something to hope for, anyhow," thought Geir.

When he came back to the camp, he melted some snow and made more soup. He sat inside the hut with Peter while they drank it and dissolved chocolate and caramels slowly in their mouths to make them last as long as possible, but their hunger was far from satisfied and seemed only to increase after tasting food.

"Ptarmigan with béchamel sauce is my favorite dish," said Peter. He began to braid snares again. "But trout in cream is also good. The prospects do not seem too bad."

"Try a cigarette," said Geir, lighting one. "They take away the worst of the hunger pangs."

Peter shook his head. "You need them more than I do," he said. "I'm not hungry enough to matter anyhow, because I have not been working. You must remember that when you divide the food."

"You need all the strength you can get to pull around," said Geir. He stubbed out his cigarette and put it away in his breast pocket. He was restless and could not stay still.

"There are still two important things that must be done," he said. "I've got to put out ground signals on the ice and also try to find the plane. I ought to see to the ground signals first, of course, but I think I'll do it the other way round so that I'm not caught by the dark."

He put two signal rockets into his pocket and gave the rest to Peter and moved his own dinghy out to the door. Just outside the door he put two armfuls of wood where Peter could reach them.

"If you aim well, you will be able to hit the fire with some of it at any rate," he said.

"Yes, I'm sure. But why can't you wait until tomorrow?"

Geir shrugged his shoulders. "It might be worse weather tomorrow," he said. "I can at any rate look around a little.

It would be fine if I could get hold of the ax and the electric torch."

"And the tobacco," said Peter with a smile.

"Yes, of course, but I'll turn around if I don't sight it within an hour's time."

He had begun to put on his snowshoes when he straightened his back and looked angrily at his watch.

"Damn," he burst out. "This wooden square will never last. I have forgotten to make myself a new showshoe."

He got hold of a cleft branch in the woodpile and went into the hut again. Peter held the ends together while Geir wound the string.

"Where do you expect to find the plane?" asked Peter.

"Four or five miles northeast from here, I think. I trimmed it practically due north."

As soon as the new snowshoe was finished, Geir prepared to set off again. He tied a cord from the dinghy round his waist and worked out his direction with a little compass from his emergency equipment. Then he said good-by and went off in a slant across the mountainside.

Toward the north the territory was rugged, and it was difficult to find a vantage point where he could get a good view over a large area. He went from height to height and kept his direction fairly accurately. He stopped on the top of each little hill and searched the area around him, and after each pause he became more eager than ever. He always thought that the chance of finding the plane from the top of the next slope was better than before.

The fact that he was hungry had its effect on his strength. His efforts began to tell on him, but this made him all the more anxious to go on. The thought of returning without having finished his task was revolting to him, for it only meant that he would have to try again the following morning. Now and again he looked at his watch. He still had time to get back before it grew dark, for he would be able to follow his own trail and could therefore walk quickly. One little hill more—then that would really have to be the last. Just as he had agreed with himself that it was now time to turn back, he saw the plane five or six hundred yards away. A shiver of joy went through him and blew away all his fatigue. There it lay, with its nose buried in the snow, on a little stretch of flat ground. It did not look as if it were badly damaged at all. The body and the wings were quite whole as far as he could see.

With renewed strength he hastened down the next slope, although another glance at the clock made him rather thoughtful. But the very clear tracks he had left in the snow gave him confidence. He would be able to follow his own trail with the flashlight even if it were dark. Once it seemed to him that he felt something wet against his face and he looked at the sky, but he could see nothing. "I probably kicked up a little snow," he thought. But before he reached the plane, snowflakes were whirling in the wind, first one or two and then many. The plain to the northwest was suddenly hidden behind closely falling snow.

Geir did not slacken his pace. He was too close. He must at any rate get the ax, the map, and the flashlight, and, if possible, the seat cushions and an extra parachute.

He bent almost double as he practically ran the last fifty yards. As he approached, he studied the plane and its tracks in the snow and noticed that it had glided on its skis for thirty to forty yards until it had tipped over nose foremost into a snowdrift.

"If we had stayed in it, I could have landed it fairly safely," he thought. "But that was impossible to know," he added to himself. "It isn't at all certain that I should either have chosen or found this landing place."

The undercarriage was bent and the propeller was splintered; otherwise, the plane looked almost undamaged. It lay sideways with its nose and one wing on the ground. The cockpit was half full of snow since both doors were lacking, but the door to the passenger compartment was fortunately closed.

Geir took off his snowshoes, climbed into the cockpit, and cleared away most of the snow with his feet. He found his tobacco pouch almost dry in a bag on the wall behind the seat, but the map had disappeared. They had left it on the seat when they had jumped out, and he supposed that it had either been blown away or lay buried under the snow. He pushed his tobacco pouch inside his jacket and opened the door to the passenger compartment. The floor slanted upwards, and he crept in on all fours. The plane rocked a little and the undercarriage sank down a little sideways into the snow. It creaked and groaned for a while; then the nose came up and the undercarriage fell back with a thud onto its tail.

Geir stood up and looked quickly round. He pulled the ax loose from its fastening on the wall and threw it out into the cockpit. Two passenger parachutes and six seat cushions followed it. That must be enough—this time at any rate. He had no time for more.

Before he left the plane, he quickly switched on the emergency electrical system and the radio, but there was no response.

When he came out from the plane, it was snowing pretty heavily and the wind had increased considerably. He hurriedly loaded the dinghy and fastened the things down securely. Small, dry, hard snowflakes whipped his face, and he had to screw up his eyes until they were almost shut in order to follow the old trail. The situation began to look very serious indeed. In three-quarters of an hour it would be quite dark, and he could scarcely expect to reach the camp in less than an hour and a half.

In the places where the ground beneath the snow was hard, the trail became less and less distinct, for the snow rounded off the edges and the light was no longer as strong as it had been. The shadows were lengthening, and it might be almost impossible to follow the trail when darkness came.

The flashlight! He had forgotten it!

He stopped. He was only about three hundred yards from the plane, so that it would be worth his while to fetch it. Or had he actually any choice? Without his flashlight he might miss the trail altogether and have to walk on and on during the whole night. He dared not take such a chance.

He left the dinghy and went quickly back to the plane. Empty-handed as he was and with the wind at his back, he reached it in a few moments and climbed up into the cockpit. He felt in the bag on the wall—but the flashlight was not there. He bit his lip, slipped down onto his knees beside the seat, and dug about in the snow. There was another bag there, and in it he found the flashlight—wet. It did not work.

Geir opened the door of the passenger compartment and sat down heavily on one of the seats. He shook the flashlight, prodded it, unscrewed it, but it was no use. Nothing did any good. Thoughtfully he gazed out at the whirling snow. The window itself was almost blocked up already. The wind had taken on a new tone, a piping sound that rose and fell, and the first signs of night had begun to appear.

With a heavy sigh he pulled out his pipe and tobacco, filled his pipe slowly and carefully before he lit it, and then lay back in the seat with his hands in his pocket. It was no use. It would be madness to set out without a flashlight and in a snowstorm.

When his pipe finally went out, he began to shiver. It was bitingly cold in the plane. He made up a bed on the floor with seat cushions and two parachutes and lay down to wait for the morning. He lay there for a long time listening to the jangling, rattling, and creaking noises in the plane while wondering in dismay how Peter would get through the night. Peter would think, no doubt, that he had lost his way in the storm.

But there was nothing—absolutely nothing—that he could do.

Seven — The Storm

After a restless night Geir woke next morning, his teeth chattering with cold. It was still dark and his watch said that it was only a quarter past five.

He jumped up, turned the chairs round, and did exercises as best he could in that narrow space. By degrees his skin began to tingle as he got his circulation going. His stomach felt as if it were touching his backbone, but there was no food in the plane, for the passenger parachutes had no dinghies attached and therefore no emergency rations.

It sounded to him as if the weather were pretty much as before, but he could see nothing as yet. It was too dark.

How in the world was he to pass the time until it grew light again? He felt his way to a seat and sat down, but soon he had to stand up again to keep warm.

If only he had had the flashlight—or a light in some form or other!

Suddenly he gave a low whistle. He had an idea—the gasoline—no, that was too dangerous. The oil! Surely he could use the lubricating oil.

There should be an empty oilcan among the tools in the baggage compartment. He felt his way to the door and fumbled on the floor and in the corners until his fingers touched cold, round metal. It was the can.

He pulled his collar well up over his ears and opened the door. Wind and snow hit him in the face, but he was able to slip out, letting the door slam behind him. Then he worked his way around the tail of the plane to the lee side, keeping close up to the body until he reached the engine. It was a little lighter outside than inside with a faint suspicion of dawn giving him enough light in which to work. He opened the cover of the engine and felt about with his hand until he found the tap of the oil filter.

When he came back again, covered with snow and frozen, he had with him a canful of oil. In the tool box he found a thick piece of twine, which he pushed down into the oil in such a way that only a little piece stuck up out of the can just like a wick.

In great excitement he struck a match. It spluttered and sparked before the oil caught fire, but when the match was almost burned out, a clear steady flame rose up from the wick. He almost shouted with joy but checked himself when he saw the flame flicker and die out. The wick burned up, and in his disappointment he stood there watching it until there was only a tiny stump left above the oil. He expected it also to die out altogether, but it did not, and when it became so short that it was able to suck up enough oil, it maintained a weak but steady flame.

Geir rubbed his hands. "I have invented the oil lamp," he said aloud to himself. "At any rate, this one!"

He looked round the compartment; there was now just

about enough light to enable him to prepare for his homeward journey.

He made a temporary rucksack out of a parachute harness together with a parachute case and took a tour of inspection around the plane looking for things that might be useful. The first-aid case and the signaling pistol were two important things that he had forgotten yesterday, and he packed them up with three red and three green signaling cartridges. Besides these, there were many odds and ends he would have liked to take with him, but he was afraid they would make his load too heavy, so he decided to leave them behind until the weather improved and he could make another trip.

He spent a quarter of an hour trying to put life into the radio as soon as it was light enough for him to see the dashboard. He examined some couplings and leads, knocked the radio and shook it wherever he could get at it, but everything was so iced up and so covered with snow that he felt he might as well give in now as later.

As soon as it was quite light, he screwed the lid onto the oilcan and packed it up with all the other things.

He opened the door and jumped out. The wind almost sent him flying, and sharp ice needles whipped his face. It was not going to be a pleasure trip—that much was certain. But he had made up his mind to go through with it, so that the sooner he got off, the better.

He stood bent double for a moment working out the direction with his compass. Yesterday he had walked just about in a northeasterly direction and therefore southwest would bring him home again. He put his compass back in his pocket and noted from which quarter he might expect the wind to come—slantwise against his right shoulder. Every cloud has a silver lining—it would be practically impossible to walk in a circle in so strong a wind.

He took about a quarter of an hour to find the rubber dinghy. First of all, he passed it without noticing it, then he turned back and began hunting for it systematically, digging up several little humps in the snow before he found the right one.

He turned the dinghy upside down to get rid of the snow, and then he tied the rucksack onto the top of the load already there and went on.

The snow swept along the ground almost horizontally, and the gusts of wind caught up the snowdrifts in boiling whirls, hitting him straight in the face. The snow stuck to his clothes in thick wet layers and filled up his eye sockets, almost blinding him. He sometimes felt as if he were walking uphill, sometimes down—it did not really matter which, for the important thing for him was to keep on in the right direction. He dared not choose the easiest way by walking round the risings for fear of losing his direction. His tracks were obliterated at once, and if he were to miss the camp now, the plane also would be lost to him. There was no way back.

He was soon exhausted, for never before in his life had his stomach been so empty. It positively ached. He could have eaten anything—just anything. "A field mouse for instance!" he thought—especially if he were allowed to grill it over his lamp. But even a field mouse would not be out and about in such devil's weather as this.

An hour passed. He looked just like a snowman. Even his face was as white as a snowdrift, for the snow had settled on his face and on the three-day-old beard.

He imagined that he ought soon to be home. He went hot all over when he thought that if he went even a few hundred yards too far to the right, he would have the hills between himself and the camp and emerge onto the plain where he had found Peter the day before. For safety's sake he altered his course a little to the left. Anything was better than getting onto the plain where there was no identifying mark of any sort. Farther east, he would in any case get some point of identification and would have a good chance of finding the lake below the camp. He could not see more than twenty to thirty yards in front of him, and it was, therefore, impossible to form a picture of the territory.

He stopped and shouted against the wind. His voice sounded thin and weak. As he listened, he realized that he would not be able to hear anything until he was quite close to the camp, for the noise of the wind was so strong that it drowned out everything else.

He trudged on.

Now and again a stormy gust of wind threatened to topple him over. These gusts became steadily wilder and wilder. He covered his face with one of his gloves and rubbed his nose now and again to see whether it still had any feeling left in it. As long as he was able to walk, he could keep himself warm enough, but his strength was ebbing out with each step. It was tempting to leave the dinghy, but after reflection he gave up the idea, for if the worst came to the worst and he was obliged to give in, the dinghy and the parachute would be the two things that would save him through the day and the night. As a last resort, he must be prepared to wrap himself up in the parachute, sit in the dinghy, fasten the cover over himself, and simply allow himself to be snowed up.

After another half hour he stopped in despair. The truth slowly dawned on him—now he was in real danger. He must have passed the camp.

"Keep calm," he whispered to himself, for he felt that panic was not far off. Now he must think coldly and calmly and make a definite plan of campaign.

He reckoned that he might have been on a level with the camp until half an hour ago. Probably he had passed north of it. He decided to walk three hundred yards due south, then northeast for half an hour, then three hundred yards south again and the same way back toward the southwest. If that did not work, he must try northwards on the same plan.

Stiff, almost rigid with cold he stumbled on again.

It made it a little easier having the wind at his back, but one of his snowshoes had split practically in half and several of the cords were broken so that one foot sank down deeper into the snow than the other. Now and again he stumbled and used up a great deal of his strength in getting up again.

He dragged himself along for another half an hour

without coming on anything that he recognized. His courage sank and his strength was almost exhausted, but he clenched his teeth and kept on moving. It was time to swing to the south. He counted about five hundred steps and stopped to rest a little before he began to grapple with the headwind again. The temptation to lie down in the snow was almost overpowering. For a moment it seemed to him that to throw himself down and really rest would be the most delicious thing he could imagine, but subconsciously he knew that it would be the last temptation he would ever know. He *must* hold out. "On!" he thought. "On, on!"

The muscles of his legs were aching and his knees were so weak that now and again they gave way under him. If he happened to sink a little deeper than usual, he fell on his knees and had to use all his will power to rise again. Each time it took him longer to get going again. His whole body cried out for rest and his mind worked more and more slowly. It was as if he stood on the border between sleeping and waking. Now and again his consciousness dimmed into a mist, and the sounds around him faded as when sleep begins to get the upper hand. He realized dimly that he had very nearly reached the borderline of what he could endure. Very soon he would have to pack himself into the rubber dinghy and settle down until he was at any rate a little rested. It sounded so simple and tempting. But how long could he hold out without food—how long would the storm last?

He turned his back to the wind and tried to rest by standing relaxed and round-shouldered with his arms hanging slackly at his side. When he could no longer hold that position, he fell on his knees, leaning his head on his arms against the dinghy. The howling of the wind changed its character. The low blustering in his ears disappeared, and he heard underlying tones, low and high pitched, rising and falling far away and close at hand. It resembled deafening, discordant organ music, and mixed in with it all was a strange, sustained whistling sound that held the one note for a long time and then suddenly stopped. He did not know when he began to notice it. He felt as if he had been hearing it for a long time as a part of all the other sounds. But by slow degrees it dawned on him that it was not part of the howling of the wind that rose and fell in an even rhythm.

There it was again.

It began suddenly, rose to full strength immediately, then stopped, as if it had been cut off with a pair of scissors.

Geir lay there immovable with his head lifted an inch or two from his arms. The slack expression on his face tightened up, and he pressed his lips together until his mouth became a thin line.

"It sounds like a whistle," he thought with amazement, "like a—like a—"

He caught his breath. Good Lord—suddenly he realized that it really *was* a whistle—one of the whistles from the emergency packs. It was Peter calling him.

His eyes filled with tears and his throat contracted. He began to sob. He lay there hunched up on his knees in the snow catching his breath and unable to get up.

After a while he pulled himself convulsively together and managed to get onto his legs. He tried to find out from which direction the piping came by walking slowly forward and turning his head first to one side, then to the other. The ground sloped slightly upwards for a little, then downward. He passed one group of small trees, then several more. He was in the birchwood on the mountain slope just above the hut.

Now Peter's whistle cut clearly and distinctly through the storm. He thought he ought to shout but had not the strength. He stumbled forward through the stunted birch trees, heaving himself forward when the dinghy stuck in the bushes. Ten yards from the hut he fell onto his knees and crawled to the entrance.

"Geir," said Peter in a hoarse voice. "Geir—what's happened to you?"

He forgot his injured leg and maneuvered himself toward Geir. Their roles were changed. Now it was Peter who arranged everything. He pulled off Geir's clothes, which were frozen stiff, and rolled him up in the parachute in which he himself had been lying and which was, therefore, warm. Then he fed Geir as if he were a baby. He gave him all the food that was left, never thinking that he himself had not tasted food since both of them had last eaten together.

While Geir lay in a doze, Peter pulled the dinghy halfway through the door opening and laboriously cleared away the snow from the dinghy itself and from its contents. It took him more than an hour to get it clean so that he could arrange a bed for himself. He laid one of the new parachutes over Geir and used the other one for himself together with the half one they already had.

He thought Geir was sleeping and lay down quietly to rest a little. He needed it. His leg was aching and his stomach still more. The knowledge that there was no more food frightened him and increased the pangs of hunger, and these pangs transplanted themselves, as it were, from his stomach into the rest of his body. His muscles felt like jelly; they trembled and shook at the least exertion.

All was quiet for a time; then Geir turned his head and looked at Peter.

"Aren't you asleep?" said Peter. "Are you warmer?"

Geir nodded. "I'm fine," he said. "I shall soon be quite all right again."

He paused and turned his eyes away. "It's due to you that I'm here, Peter," he said.

Peter did not answer. A new, warm note had crept into Geir's voice, and the cold, impersonal tone had vanished. It seemed as if something in the very atmosphere between them was changed. Peter felt it himself and he sensed that the feeling was mutual.

"I should have hunted toward the north, in quite the wrong direction, if I hadn't heard your whistle," said Geir, his eyes fixed on the twigged roof. "That is to say, if I had had the strength to go any further. I was absolutely finished. I had no will power left, had no wish but to lie down in the snow and die! You—"

"Then we're quits," Peter broke in. "One each!"

Geir shut his eyes and smiled absently. Then he turned suddenly toward Peter and looked at him searchingly.

"You're speaking very indistinctly," he said. "Is there anything wrong with your mouth?"

"It's a little sore," answered Peter. "I suppose I can't stand the cold."

Geir raised himself on his elbow. "Tell me," he said slowly, "how long had you been blowing that whistle?"

Peter shrugged his shoulders and turned away. The corners of his mouth trembled suspiciously.

"Since six o'clock last night," he mumbled thickly.

Eight — Hunger

The next day the storm raged as angrily as ever, if not worse. Both the boys woke early before it was light and lay throwing themselves restlessly backwards and forwards and turning from side to side without being able to get to sleep again.

At last Geir half rose and groaned. "Goodness, what a head I've got!"

"You, too?" said Peter. "My head feels like splitting any moment."

In a twinkling Geir was over by the door and digging like a maniac in the snow.

"We're snowed in," he said with a groan. "The door and our air hole are both snowed up. We've used up all the oxygen in here."

The snow was packed hard in front of the entrance, and it took Geir a little while to clear a hole. Then the cold fresh air streamed in, and they drank it in like a refreshing drink. After that they quickly revived and their headaches disappeared.

A faint streak of light filtered in through the door. Dawn was not far off.

Geir lay down and stretched himself until his joints cracked. "I feel like a new person," he said. "As if I've been ill and now I'm well again. I'm only a little stiff and my stomach feels quite hollow. How's yours?"

"Like my bank account the day before I get my pay check," said Peter.

"Have we any food left?"

"Not as much as a crumb."

They laughed a little and pondered on the situation, looking out into the half darkness. The snow whirled past the door in a wild witches' dance. The little space outside that Geir had cleared had filled up almost halfway to the door.

"I could eat the soles off my shoes if I could cook them," said Peter.

"We may come to that," said Geir. He dragged his home-made rucksack toward him and showed what he had brought. The oil lamp filled him with the greatest pride. He sat on his heels on the floor and took off the lid.

"Give me the soles," he said. He struck a match and lighted the wick.

"We're getting on," said Peter. "If you go on furnishing the hut and getting hold of any more kitchen utensils, *and* we get something to cook, we can settle down here forever, except for—"

"What?"

"Oh, I just thought of our people at home sitting and waiting for news. They won't be feeling very happy, I'm afraid. Probably they don't sleep as well nights as we do."

"No."

Geir sat there filling his pipe. He stopped and looked thoughtfully in front of him; then he went on filling it without speaking. They had said all that could be said about that matter.

They lay for another half an hour chatting about yesterday's experiences. Geir told Peter about his unsuccessful attempt to get the radio going, about the flashlight and the icy night in the plane, and the journey home.

Peter had not much to tell, but lay there enjoying the confidential manner in which Geir told his story. Geir did not try to cover up his mistakes and never excused himself, and he asked Peter's advice in planning the coming day and about what they must do if the snowstorm still went on. From now on they would discuss everything together.

Geir suddenly started up as if he had just come to his senses and unwound himself from the parachute.

"It's light," he said, and began to put on his boots. "How long do you think the snares had been set before the storm began?"

"About five hours, I should say."

"Do you think there's any chance?"

"Dead sure. I'll put on the saucepan while you're away if you will fill it with snow before you go."

"O.K. I'll be back with our steaks in ten minutes."

The loose snow was heavy to walk in, and the wind kept pushing Geir sideways so that now and again he was obliged to give a clumsy jump in order to keep his balance. It was more sheltered in the little wood. He found no difficulty in picking out the places where he had set the snares, but they were quite snowed under. He had to dig his way down to the tops of the branches and feel his way along to the entrances and the slipknots. He moved from entrance to entrance. The nooses lay at half an arm's length down in the snow, and most of them had become twisted round the twigs by the wind. Alas! There was not much hope.

Nevertheless, his heart beat more quickly every time he rummaged about in the snow around the entrance to one of the snares. After all, there was always a small possibility—

Suddenly he felt an icy lump in his hand. His arm became quite numb and trembling, and the blood shot up into his face until his skin tingled. He got up and stared skeptically at the white lump in his hand, his mouth half open as if he could scarcely believe his eyes. It was a fully-grown ptarmigan.

His first instinct was to shout and rush back to the hut, but then he pulled himself together and examined the last remaining snares. They were all empty. He half ran down the slope, stumbled, and got up again, rushed up to the door of the hut looking like a snowman, and threw the ptarmigan into Peter's lap.

"Is it really real?" shouted Peter, and looked at it almost suspiciously, but it did not take long for him to realize that they had food—real, solid food, roast ptarmigan.

Peter had made a stand of thick branches around the lamp on which to put the saucepan, and before long the snow melting had been started. But the heat was too weak, and even after some time they could not see any difference in the level of the snow in the cooking vessel.

Geir extinguished the lamp and fitted three new wicks into the oil. This helped a lot, but it still seemed to take an endless time for the water to boil. The ptarmigan was plucked and cleaned and cut up into small pieces long before the water was half warm.

When the smell of boiled ptarmigan at last began to tickle their nostrils, they endured almost unbearable tortures. They had to exert every ounce of self-control while they waited for the stew to be ready.

But then they had a meal that they never forgot. They ate up everything to the last bit, even to chewing the bones and drinking the water in which the ptarmigan had been boiled. The best meal either of them had ever tasted could not compare with this one.

Afterwards they lay down and relaxed. Geir puffed contentedly at his pipe, but it was not long before Peter began to perspire and feel very ill. He said nothing, but his face grew pale and turned greener and greener. Finally he sat up and hastily snatched at the cooking vessel.

Geir turned and looked at him anxiously when he saw that he was throwing up all the food he had eaten. Heart-rending though it was, Geir had to go out and throw away into the snow the half-digested food in its green slime.

When he came back again, he sat for a long time gazing inquiringly at Peter, who lay there with his eyes closed, half moaning.

"How much of the chocolate that was left did you eat while I was away?" he asked darkly.

"I can't remember, a bar or two perhaps. Don't speak to me about food." Peter moaned.

"I want to know; don't lie," said Geir sternly.

Peter did not answer.

"The trouble is that you ate nothing at all," said Geir. "You gave it all to me. I was too worn out to notice, but I remember now that I ate for a long time."

Peter only threw his arms over his eyes and moaned.

"If you think you did me a service, you're mistaken. What do you want me to do now?"

Depair and anger fought for the upper hand in Geir's mind. He lay down on his back and stared up at the roof, his lips pressed together into a hard line, but by degrees his expression grew kinder. There was silence in the hut. Peter was breathing heavily but had stopped groaning.

"Forgive me," said Geir. He rose and began to fiddle with the lamp. "I will melt a little water for you," he said heavily. "We'll hope the weather will soon improve."

But it did not improve. The storm continued without stopping for all that day and the next. To begin with, they busied themselves knotting the fishing lines, and Geir made himself some new, larger, and stronger snowshoes. Then they slept a good deal, but after a time when hunger again began to gnaw at their innards, there was not much sleep either.

Finally Peter was so weak that he lay in a semi-doze and seemed quite indifferent to everything. His feeling of hunger diminished by degrees, but there was no strength left in him. His muscles refused to obey him, and he remained in the same position all the time, gazing up at the ceiling when he was not sleeping. Geir grew more and more restless.

Outside the hut the storm raged ceaselessly. It was as if the whole world was in turmoil. The snow whirled round and round like white foam over the moors, and it was useless to set snares and impossible to get down to the ice to fish.

The snow piled up outside the hut and it drifted up over the windscreen and down on the lee side so that there was nothing but a mild slope from the windscreen to the other end of the yard. The hut had lost its outlines altogether and looked like nothing but a huge heap of snow. It was fairly flat on top, for Geir went out now and again and swept away the worst, since there were limits to the amount the roof could stand. But he allowed it to heap up along the walls, which became so tightly packed that the hut was quite warm and cozy even though they had to do without a fire. It is true enough that every cloud has a silver lining.

On the third day Geir got up resolutely and dressed. Peter lay there, pale and slack, half asleep. He did not even turn his head when Geir went out.

Before he put on his leather jacket, Geir made a protective mask against the whirling snow for his face. He cut holes for his eyes and his nose in a piece of parachute silk and tied it over his head, securing it round his neck with his scarf. With his leather coat and his cap on the top of his mask, he thought he was well protected against the hard icy needles that the storm swept along the ground.

He took the plywood square under his arm and sneaked out without waking Peter, who in his present weak condition might have had a shock if he had suddenly seen such a white ghostlike face.

After almost half an hour's struggle through the loose snow Geir had crossed the wood and was out on the moor walking more or less in the same direction as when he went to look for the plane. This time he did not go far. In a sheltered nook on the lee side of a little hill he stopped and began to hunt among the snowdrifts until he found a spot where the snow did not seem to be so deep. It was just below the summit of the hill, and the snow must have been blown past it and collected in drifts a little lower down.

He began to dig. The top snow was light and dry, and the wind helped him by blowing it away when he threw it into the air, but new snow slid down into the hole almost as quickly as he shoveled the old away. He seemed to be getting nowhere. Nevertheless, he went on working steadily and evenly, but slowly so that he might not get too hot. The hole grew gradually larger and by degrees took on the shape of a funnel with a top circumference of several yards.

When he reached firmer snow, he cut blocks and stacked them up as a windscreen behind him. Everything became calmer immediately. He dug down vertically just behind the wall so that the snow should not fall in so easily, and the digging went more and more quickly the deeper he got.

After a couple of hours' work the plywood square struck bare ground. He worked on shoveling feverishly. Small bits of earth and tufts of moss began to appear mixed in with the snow, and he stopped suddenly. He knelt down and gazed intently at the bits of moss. Was it reindeer moss? At any rate, it was not like any other moss that he had ever seen before, and that might be taken as proof enough. It consisted of a network of fine gray threads and felt soft and spongy in his hand. He put a piece into his mouth to taste it and chewed hard. The moss tasted of nothing at all, but he could not resist swallowing it. He put more into his mouth. Reindeer moss was food, food for reindeer and for starving people. It contained nourishment; more than that he could not say.

He had to force himself to stop eating, for he was not sure that reindeer moss could be eaten raw. In the section in the Air Force Handbook dealing with lifesaving, it was mentioned among the herbs that should be cooked.

The vegetation was very scarce at the place he had chosen, but he found enough to satisfy their worst hunger. When he left, all his pockets were full.

Peter started and smiled weakly when Geir came into the hut with the frosted mask over his face. Two long icicles hung below his nostrils, looking like tusks.

"Now we're going to do some cooking," shouted Geir gaily, and threw off his jacket. "I can't promise you a grand meal, but it will give us enough strength to ride the storm. It shan't get us down as long as we have reindeer moss!"

He felt in his pockets and held out two fistfuls toward Peter.

"Is it edible?" asked Peter. He actually turned his head to look.

"Is it edible? It's full of vitamins and calories. It's one of the Lapps' favorite dishes."

"If they have nothing else to eat," he added to himself.

Nine — The Storm Dies Down

Geir lit the lamp, filled the cooking vessel with snow, and put it on. He rubbed his hands together in a contented way and talked gaily.

Peter turned over on his side and watched the snow-melting operation, and by degrees more life came into the pale face. But he did not seem inclined to talk. His eyes looked strangely large and clear, and they stood out in sharp contrast to the dark shadows under them.

At long last the water came to a boil. Geir had cleaned the reindeer moss thoroughly, so that it was free from all earth, and he now threw three handfuls into the boiling water. He peeled the bark off a stick and used it to stir the mixture round and round until the moss sank to the bottom. By degrees it began to dissolve, and the water became as thick as soup. He went on stirring, took a taste from the stick, and smacked his lips thoughtfully. The taste was not much to boast about—rather bitter—but the mere feeling of something edible in his mouth affected him so strongly that he found it difficult to wait for more.

Peter had shut his eyes again and lay in a half-doze.

Geir kept looking at him anxiously while he went on stirring. Suddenly he blew the steam aside to see how the soup was getting on. When he finally lifted the cooking vessel off the heat and put out the lamp, the moss was almost dissolved and the water was thick and like a jelly. "Food," he shouted, and poured a few mouthfuls into Peter's cooking vessel.

He sat down beside Peter, put his arm under Peter's shoulders to support him, and held the cooking vessel to his mouth. Peter gulped down a mouthful and then looked at Geir in an astonished sort of way. Geir gave him an encouraging smile in return. Then Peter stretched out his mouth for more, and Geir gave him five mouthfuls.

"That's enough for the moment," said Geir. "I'll give you a double lot in half an hour's time. How do you like it?"

"It's fine," said Peter. Then he dozed off again.

Geir drank slowly. He longed to put the cooking vessel to his mouth and swallow it all down at once, but he knew it would only come up again unless his stomach had time to accustom itself slowly to work, for it had had too long a rest.

Peter improved throughout the day. Geir made some more soup every half hour or warmed up what was left and gave him larger and larger helpings. The color began to return to his cheeks, and he woke up from his half-doze. He improved more quickly than either of them had thought possible, and when he fell asleep toward evening, he was breathing calmly and regularly. The danger had passed.

It was not snowing the next morning, but the storm and

the drifting snow were still there even if possibly it had abated. They drank their breakfast soup and waited about a little, but Geir was restless. He had begun to hope again. Perhaps the worst would soon be over.

By degrees they noticed a lull in the weather, and between eleven and twelve Geir set off with the plywood square and the ax. He had long ago determined the best place for fishing, namely the mouth of a small stream not far from the hut. The stream itself was now dried up, but he reckoned that the ice there would be thinner as a current probably ran there when first the frost came.

He dug down in the same way as when he was hunting for reindeer moss. The snow on the ground was deeper and the drifting snow more difficult than he had expected, but when he had once got his windscreen up, the work progressed more quickly. Hour after hour passed. The fishing line was two and a half yards long, and he had, of course, to clear a longer space than this. Many shovelsful of snow had to be shoveled away; many blocks had to be cut out and lifted up onto the wall. But at last he was able to lay aside his plywood square and pick up the ax.

It drew toward evening before he had got through at two places and had made one hole big enough to push a branch slantwise under the ice toward the other hole. He fetched the tackle from the hut and selected a long, bent birch stick from the snow-covered heap of branches outside the hut. Back on the ice he stripped the branch of twigs and measured it between the holes. It reached. He tied a long string onto the thin edge of the stick and pushed it slantwise through the hole. The difficulty lay in steering the branch in such a way that it floated up toward the ice exactly beneath the other hole. Unfortunately, his arm did not reach down far enough beneath the edge of the ice, nor was the cold water particularly tempting.

After some thought he went up to the hut again and fetched a cleft branch, which he tied loosely to the thick end of the stick. Then he was able to push the stick right under the ice and hoped it would float up toward the underside of the ice. He was lucky. The point stopped just below the other hole, and after juggling a little with the branch, he was able to see it down in the water. He got hold of the string with a twig and drew it toward him. Now there was a connection between the holes, and the rest was as easy as winking. He fastened the line to the string, pulled it down under the ice, and tied the ends to twigs, which he fastened securely in the snow.

Not until now did he notice that it was beginning to get dark and that he was cold and tired. He had meant to stay until there were fish on the line, but after a few minutes he was shivering so much that he gave in. Besides, he could not see, partly because darkness was falling very rapidly and partly because the drifting snow was hiding everything. There was nothing to be done—he must wait until morning.

When Geir got home, Peter had the reindeer-moss soup ready. Geir peeled off his outer clothes that were frozen stiff and rolled himself up in the parachute. The warm cooking vessel in his hands and the scalding soup in his stomach soon worked a miracle in his frozen body.

"Isn't this good," he said, and gave a deep sigh of satisfaction. "This is better than walking into the mess on a bitterly cold winter's day and eating cutlets, creamed rice, coffee and cakes, even if the mess and its cutlets are better than our hut and its soup. It's not that that is important. The feeling of well-being depends on the connection between what you come from and what you come to."

"Quite right," said Peter. "It agrees with the theory of relativity anyhow. Do you think we'll get some fish?"

"Dead certain," said Geir. "There's not a lake on the Finnmark Moors that isn't overpopulated. And the fish up here have never seen fishing tackle before, so they'll all queue up to inspect the strange thing that has got under the ice somehow. There's sure to be fish, good fat trout, if I'm not mistaken—as soon as I've cleared my way down to the lake tomorrow morning."

"You're a wonder," said Peter. "Tomorrow evening at this time all our troubles will be over. We shall be eating good strong fish-soup and lightly boiled fillet of trout."

"We'll have it for breakfast," said Geir positively. "I do believe the wind is really subsiding."

Geir's expectations proved correct. They woke in the morning with a wonderful realization of a deep silence all around them. Geir lay listening to it in astonishment. Then he jumped up and knelt in front of the opening. The air was clear and still. The clouds sailed gently and quietly across the sky, but they still lay low over the mountains.

Peter had raised himself on his elbows. "You were right," he said smiling. "Shall I put on the water?"

"Yes, do"—Geir hesitated a little—"in about half an

hour's time. I expect I shall have to clear away some drift snow first."

It was a joy to get out and to be able to stretch his body and draw in his breath without being half suffocated by the wind. Geir felt as if he had lain, stood, and walked bent double from time immemorial. He whistled contentedly while he pottered down toward the fishing place, but as he approached it, his excitement gained the upper hand and he stopped whistling.

There was less snow in the hole than he had dared to hope, and after scarcely a quarter of an hour's shoveling, he managed to get hold of the string at one of the holes. He pulled at it carefully. A shiver of excitement went through him when he felt a feeble trembling on the line. It was fish—at any rate one. If only he did not lose it!

Feverishly he shoveled the snow aside at the other end of the string. He did not give himself time to dig right down but pushed his arm in until he got hold of the twig and loosened the string.

He leaped back to the other hole again, knelt down, and brushed aside the rest of the snow with his hands so energetically that it surrounded him like dust. Then he was able to pull up the line and saw there were fish in it. In his excitement he danced a regular war dance, shouting up toward the hut like a lunatic. There were three trout, one big three-quarter pounder and two rather smaller ones.

He pushed the line back into the hole to prevent it from freezing stiff, but it was quite out of the question to take time to rig it up properly just then. He was far too excited and anxious to get back to the hut and to Peter. He seized the knife, and in two quick slashes he ripped the fish open and cleaned them. Then he began to run toward the hut where Peter was busily melting the snow.

What a feast they had! Nothing in the world could possibly have tasted as good as boiled trout and no drink could be better than hot fish-water. They ate everything, skin, bones, head, bag and baggage, and any prickings of conscience they might have had because they kept nothing till later, they drowned in gay chatter. They wanted to satisfy their hunger once and for all—and they did.

Afterwards they felt such a feeling of well-being and such a healthy sleepiness that even Geir allowed himself half an hour's rest.

Afterwards he began on the day's work with renewed strength. He laid out the lines again, rigged up twelve snares, cleared the yard, dug out the fireplace, cleared away the snow from the woodpile, and lit a flaming campfire. Finally he brought five or six loads of wood to the camp.

By evening everything was finished.

The temperature inside the hut had risen to such an extent that Geir decided that now was the time to wash socks and underclothes. He knew that clothes that have been saturated with sweat do not hold the warmth.

They rubbed themselves down with pieces of parachute silk and put on their Guernsey shirts next to their skin. Geir made himself slippers from parachute silk, pulled on his boots, and rushed down to the fishing place where he rinsed the clothes in ice-cold water.

The line was empty. A little disappointed, he returned to the hut and set out the clothes to dry by the fire. Perhaps it had been rather rash to eat up all the fish so quickly.

"You might try spearing the fish by lamplight this evening!" suggested Peter. "If you can find anything to spear them with!"

"Perhaps," answered Geir thoughtfully. "But to do that, I should have to have a pretty big hole. What do you say to making a new hole and luring the fish to the line with the lamp?"

"Most ingenious!" said Peter.

By dusk Geir had everything ready for a big fishing venture. He had cleared the hole in the ice of snow and enlarged it so that there was a place for the third hole between the two old ones and about three feet nearer land. When it grew dark, he went to fetch the lamp but on his way he realized that the light from it would be too weak to penetrate down under the ice, so he took down with him instead an armful of wood and lit a campfire on the ice. This was an advantage in other ways as well—it kept him warm while he was waiting.

Ten minutes had not passed before the line began to shake and tremble. He pulled it in triumphantly and landed two fine trout straight away. This was indeed fishing on the grand scale. The food problem was solved once and for all. Obviously the lake was simply swarming with fish. Perhaps the Finnmark Moor was not, after all, the worst place in the world in which to be wrecked.

Five minutes later he had caught a few more fish, but he left the line. The earlier tremblings turned into powerful tugs and jerks, and he had to fix the branches more firmly in the snow. When he at last decided to pull up the line, he had altogether six trout, both large and small.

It began to get very cold. "That better be enough for tonight," he thought, for he knew that their hunger cure was over. He put out the line again, extinguished the fire, and went home.

"Did you ever see anything like it!" exclaimed Peter.

Ten — Visitors from the Wilds

The days passed.

The weather remained unchanged as did life in the camp. Geir kept the fire going always, and the stone wall at the back of the hut became so warm that the temperature inside the hut remained even and comfortable. They were no longer obliged to wear their outdoor things in the hut while washing their vests and stockings, and their beds with the cushions from the plane as mattresses were warmer and softer.

Food supplies had increased so that they were now able to have two or three satisfactory meals a day. They had more fish than they could eat, and now and again there was a ptarmigan in the snares that Geir put out. Geir made an icebox outside the hut, and there they kept the fish and ptarmigan when they had been cleaned and readied for cooking.

Life in the wilderness had become quite pleasant.

But the clouds did not lift. They lay low and heavy over the mountains and the moors and were gray, almost black.

Geir had not so much to do any longer. He spent one day making an enormous SOS of branches, which he laid out on the ice, but when that was finished, he had only the daily routine work to do. He collected wood, cooked food, and examined the fishing lines and the snares morning and evening.

He sat for hours brooding over the fact that they had not yet been found and wondering why this was. He had now no doubt in his mind that they had given a wrong position; otherwise, the helicopter or the patrol from Alta or Kautokeino would surely have found them during the days that had passed since the storm subsided. It was difficult to understand that they were right outside the district that must by now have been searched, but without a map it was impossible for him to reckon the extent of the mistake that he had made. He simply had no idea where they were.

One bitter cold night Geir woke because he was shivering. The fire had nearly burned itself out, and he leaned forward toward the door and threw on a few branches. He remained in that position for some moments to make sure that the fire burned up.

Suddenly he heard a noise from the darkness. He could not say what it was, but it was at any rate something different from the soft sighing of the wind and the crackling of the fire. He listened for a moment, every nerve stretched, but the sound was not repeated.

"It must have been something—I'm absolutely sure of that," he thought. "It sounded almost like a shout."

He was now wide awake, but as he had heard nothing for three or four minutes, he lay back in his dinghy and lit his pipe. He drew in the smoke slowly so that he might not be disturbed by the sucking noise in the mouthpiece should the sound come again.

There! There it was again, far away—a shout. It must be a shout.

"Peter!" he yelled. "Peter!"

He unrolled himself quickly from his parachute and pushed his feet into his boots.

"They're coming! We're saved!" he cried, deeply moved.

Peter sat bolt upright, his face a mixture of sleepy confusion and wide-awake expectation.

"Is it true?" he burst out. He looked through the door opening. "Now? In the middle of the night?"

"Sure," said Geir. "They shouted. I heard it clearly—far away."

He wriggled out of the door and stood up beside the fire.

"Ahoy!" he shouted out into the darkness. "A-hoy! A-hoy!"

They held their breath waiting for an answer. Peter had crawled toward the door and lay with his head just outside it. They listened eagerly for a minute or two. Then Geir shouted again, cupping his mouth with his hands and shouting in all directions.

But the night remained quite silent, except for the faint soughing of the wind and the crackling of the fire.

"You must have dreamed it," said Peter, disappointed.

"Dreamed?" said Geir. "I was as wide awake as I am now. I had made up the fire and was going to smoke just because I was so wide awake. I heard it twice."

Geir shouted again, but still all was quiet. "The shouts may have come with the wind," he said. "And *mine* don't carry against it. I must stand against it. I must stand against the wind and shout until I get an answer."

He fetched his snowshoes and bent down to put them on. Then they both heard it again—a long drawn-out howl that rose and sank as if it were carried on an uneven wind.

Geir arose. "Did you hear it?" he whispered.

"Stand still!" cried Peter sharply. "Stand still! Don't shout!"

Something in Peter's voice made Geir pause and listen. A minute passed. Then they heard it again as if it were nearer.

The boys did not move for a long time. There was no longer any doubt. That was not a human voice.

"Wolves," said Peter firmly.

Geir did not answer. Disappointment and horror were written all over his face. Involuntarily he raised his head and scanned the heavens in all directions, but he only saw darkness—not so much as an indication of a star. Flying weather was as far away as ever, and the same applied to help. He took off his snowshoes and came back into the hut. Without saying a word, he began to clean the snow off his boots with a twig.

"Brrr! What a horrible sound!" said Peter. "But they say that wolves are quite harmless nowadays unless they are desperate with hunger."

"Yes, they are too cowardly," said Geir confidently. "Even when they're hungry, they only attack in large packs so that they are quite sure of victory. Besides, I haven't heard of anyone being killed by a wolf in our lifetime. That sort of thing only happened in olden days."

"I've heard so too. But how that can be I can't imagine. Surely wolves don't change their nature in such a short time."

Geir shrugged his shoulders.

"Perhaps they hunted in larger packs because there were more of them?"

"Don't ask me! As far as I know, they may have planned to have us for their breakfast, but I'm sure our fire will dispel their courage."

Geir was silent. A long, dismal howl struck sharply through the darkness. It rose to a high trembling note and fell to silence slowly and mournfully. Immediately afterwards came one more from another direction, but apparently at about the same distance. The sounds were much nearer than before.

"There are at least two," said Peter. His voice sounded strained.

"More, I'm afraid," announced Geir. "I think they would have been more careful if there had been only two. If there are only one or two, they only hunt small game and disappear as soon as they scent danger."

Peter cleared his throat and laughed uncertainly. "I wonder what they call us? Big game?"

He got no reply, and the conversation languished. They both lay dead quiet but heard nothing more. The feeling of horror mounted within them as they realized that the wolves, for all they knew, might be quite close.

The fire fell in and sent up a rain of sparks into the darkness. Geir leaned forward and threw on another branch. As he stretched out his hand to pick up one more, he suddenly stiffened, screwed up his eyes, and blinked incredulously toward the wall of blackness beyond the fire.

"Look!" he whispered without moving. "To the left, over there!"

Peter leaned toward the door and looked in the same direction. His heart thumped so loudly that it sounded to him like heavy drumbeats getting faster and faster. Right opposite him he distinguished two shining points. They disappeared for a moment and then reappeared again. They were two eyes shining like glowing coals in the darkness.

"There's another one," whispered Geir. "Two more—no, a whole pack."

The wolves were standing in a half circle about fifty yards from the campfire. The fire dazzled the two fliers so that they saw nothing but the animals' eyes and heard not a sound except their own heavy breathing. Neither of them dared to move. The men on one side of the fire and the wolves on the other stared at each other as if bewitched.

The minutes crawled along. Neither Geir nor Peter could say afterwards how long it lasted, but they reckoned that the first streak of dawn must have appeared on the horizon about half an hour later. Then the wolves disappeared as noiselessly as they had come. But long after it had grown quite light, the two fliers sat there spellbound, not knowing what to set about first.

"Goodness, how hungry I am!" came at last almost like a sigh from Peter.

That loosened the tension, and Geir began to smile. He slipped out of the door and looked round in all directions but apart from the tracks in the snow there was nothing to remind him of the night's horror.

"They were ghosts," said Peter, "and they have disintegrated."

"Ghosts don't leave tracks in the snow," said Geir. He threw wood on the fire and put the cooking vessel on the embers. When the snow had melted, he cut up three small trout and put them in the water.

"Well, that was actually a very exciting experience—now that it's over," said Peter. "I suppose they're miles away by now. I don't begrudge them anything, but all the same I can't but hope they will find some really satisfying food before tonight."

"I hope so too," said Geir. "But we'll have to be prepared for another visit tonight, so I think I'll spend most of the day collecting plenty of firewood."

He tried to reckon from the tracks how many animals there had been, but in vain. The slope leading down toward the lake was trampled fairly tightly, but on the ice he could count what looked like ten to twelve different tracks. Some of them could of course have been the same wolf, so that he guessed there might have been between eight and ten of them in all.

When he came back, the trout were cooked, and they divided the food without saying a word until their hunger was satisfied.

"Is your leg knitting all right, do you think?" asked Geir after a while.

"I can hear it growing," said Peter. "Now I can wriggle my big toe without feeling it in my forefinger. If it goes on like this, we shall be able to walk home in a week or two because obviously no one is going to fetch us. I am beginning to think that they have given us up."

"Are you crazy?" said Geir. "They won't give us up as long as there is a ghost of a chance that we are still alive, and there must be that because we *are* still alive."

"But why haven't they found us then?" said Peter impatiently. "The helicopter has had flying weather for two or three days, and the patrols could have been out for four."

"The position we gave them may have been absolutely wrong," said Geir. "I can't imagine why, and at any rate I can't understand how it could have been as far out as all that. Though—"

"Though—?"

"Well, perhaps we weren't so far out after all. Such strange things can happen. Those who are organizing the search usually know so little to begin with and they think and reason things out and try to discover where the fault in position lies, and their very reasoning may lead them astray."

He held out the palm of his hand and began to draw in it with his finger.

"Let us say that the position we gave them is here by my thumb. They drew a circle round it with a radius of 10 to 15 per cent of the stretch we flew from the last position we reported before we went above the clouds. They have searched that circle from end to end, and it may well be that we are *just* outside it. But instead of enlarging the circle, they have perhaps reasoned themselves into a more obvious mistake—that they have misunderstood the radio message, or something of that sort. I cannot remember what position we gave them, but say that we reported 23° 15′ East. They may perhaps suspect that we said 50′, because fifteen and fifty can easily be mixed up. Then they draw a new circle round 23° 50′ and search where the two circles do not cut each other. All this takes time. Then they think out new theories. But they won't give up—until they chance to find the right one—of that we can be sure!"

They gulped down the boiling fish-water and Geir got up. "I'm going to cut wood for five or six hours," he said.

"Take the signal pistol with you," suggested Peter. "It will not be much good as a hunting weapon, but it may be pretty useful for frightening them away."

"Oh, they'll keep far away in daylight," said Geir. "But I'll take the pistol anyhow, just in case the helicopter might lose its way in this direction."

During the course of the day he dragged an enormous pile of wood to the camp. He cut up the branches into small bits and stacked the smaller pieces at the side of the door so that they could easily reach them from inside. In a pause to rest, he examined the snares and found a ptarmigan, which he plucked and prepared for the icebox. But the line was empty for once. It was the first morning there had been no fish.

As it drew toward evening, the wood heap was over three feet high, and there was no more room along the wall of the hut. The rest of the day was used by Geir to plant a branch fence in the snow round the yard. It was soon about two feet high, but rather thin and weak. It would be no real protection against the wolves, but it might frighten them because it made a boundary between the darkness and the light shed by the fire.

A new visit to the lake gave them a couple of small fish, and Geir was satisfied with his day's work and took off his snowshoes. He found a pointed stick and hung a ptarmigan over the embers before he took off his outer clothes and threw himself down on his bunk with a deep sigh.

"What shall we have for dinner today?" said Peter. "Meat soup and ptarmigan, or fish soup and trout?"

"Only ptarmigan," said Geir. "Barbecued ptarmigan for a change."

Eleven — Besieged

Dusk fell while they were still eating their supper. Darkness obliterated detail after detail, and the night came in over the horizon until it stood like a thick wall behind the campfire. And with the darkness came anxiety and tension. The evening was uncommonly silent and still.

But the time passed and nothing happened. Their hope of a quiet night grew stronger by degrees, but the suspense was too great to allow them to sleep to begin with. They each remained sitting in their dinghys with their eyes fixed on the door.

They talked but only intermittently, for each of them had his own thoughts. Now and again Geir threw a branch onto the fire. By the time it was ten o'clock the work of the day and the short previous night began to tell on Geir. His eyelids grew heavy and he fell into an uneasy sleep. Peter lay down and he also shut his eyes, but he was not tired. He had dozed once or twice during the day and had in that way made up for the loss of sleep during the night. Anxiety was enough to keep him awake, and he opened his eyes and looked out through the door into the darkness at least every half minute.

Just after midnight they both started up with a jerk and looked uncertainly toward each other. The heavy silence was broken by a long, doleful howl only two or three hundred yards away from the hut. Almost immediately it was answered from another quarter by another howl, and then another, howl upon howl, calling to each other and answering out there in the darkness.

There was something intensely dismal in the way the howls died away. The sound reached its highest note and then sank down slowly through the scale with a wailing undertone that was almost human and that penetrated bone and marrow. Although Geir and Peter had, of course, never heard it before, they could guess that this was the hunger howl of the wolves. Such despairing sounds could only come from beings who felt themselves threatened by deadly peril, and for wild animals the threat of death by starvation is more terrifying than anything else.

Without saying anything to each other, they both realized at once that this night was going to be more frightening and perhaps more dangerous than the last. When the shining eyes began to ring them around again, it was not done as silently as before. Low, suppressed growls indicated that the wolves were much more impatient than before.

They advanced almost to the branch fence. Geir regretted that he had made it since when all was said and done, perhaps they felt safer when they had something tangible between themselves and the fire.

The pack was restless. Their eyes glowed for a time and then disappeared and reappeared at another place. When

Geir and Peter held their breath, they could hear the pat-pat of the wolves' feet in the snow and again and then again a low growl. Every time Geir banked up the fire or threw on more wood, they drew back, but a moment afterwards they were in their places again, a little nearer—always a little nearer.

"What are they waiting for?" said Peter, when half an hour had passed. "Do they think we'll go for a walk in the middle of the night?"

"I suppose they think nothing at all," said Geir. "They are afraid of the fire but are so desperate with hunger that they can't tear themselves away from the sight of the delicious food on the other side of it."

"What word did you say?" asked Peter.

"Food," shouted Geir. "Us!"

After a time they were able to make out dark shadows behind the glittering eyes. The ring came nearer. Sometimes they glimpsed white teeth.

Peter shivered. "Stoke up, for goodness' sake," he said. "This is beyond a joke."

Geir nodded and bent forward to pick up a piece of wood, but that was as far as he got. His whole body suddenly stiffened and remained paralyzed. He was staring straight into the eyes of a wolf who had got inside the branch hedge and stood four or five yards to the left of the door, half hidden by the stack of wood. The wolf, looking like a shaggy, starved dog stood with its mouth open and its teeth gleaming white in the light of the fire. It looked as if it were growling, although not a sound could be heard.

The whole episode lasted for about a second. Then the wolf disappeared again into the darkness. But the sight had burned itself into Geir's consciousness. He stared speechless in the direction in which the wolf had gone. It was not until a good while afterwards, when the feeling of paralysis had left him at last, that he caught hold of a burning branch and hurled it out into the darkness.

As if they had been given a signal, the whole pack were set in motion. They drew back a little way and then one of them began to howl. In an instant the air trembled with a chorus of wild voices. The sounds seemed to come from all sides, both above and below the hut. The boys sat listening, stiff with fright. Involuntarily they pressed themselves against the back wall of the hut to get as far away from the door as possible. By degrees all was silent again, but the ring stood there as before, watchful and waiting.

Geir threw more and more wood on the fire, so much, in fact, that it flared up and became much broader. Smoke seeped into the hut, but it settled under the roof and did not trouble them much. The brightness of the fire blinded them and they could see less than before, but it made them feel more secure as the door opening was better covered.

It seemed to them as if one particular wolf always came nearer the fire than the others. Suddenly they would see it within the circle of light, sneaking along, its head close to the ground, its back bent ready to spring. This wolf was apparently the leader of the pack.

They tried to keep an eye on it, but it was always moving, in and out of the circle of light, turning up in unexpected places.

"If that chap goes crazy and jumps across the fire at us, the others will follow blindly," said Geir. "That's all it needs—that one of them shall go mad. I wonder how far hunger can drive them."

"Well," said Peter, "I don't know if one can compare animals and people, but I can't remember that either you or I were anywhere near going off our heads when our hunger was at its greatest."

Geir shrugged his shoulders.

"I am not so sure," he said. "How do you think we would have felt if we had been sitting outside a snowhut full of, shall we say, cutlets and steaks?"

Peter looked at him almost terrified. He scratched his head thoughtfully and then he burst out, "You make me feel as if they are very stupid if they don't get at us pretty soon. How many of them do you think there are?"

"At least eight, perhaps ten or twelve. I can't say exactly."

"It's now half-past two, four hours to dawn. Shall we try to frighten them with a few shots from the signal pistol?"

"Daren't! You saw how the burning branch worked them up. When they begin to howl in chorus, they are bravest. The more they are welded together, the more dangerous they are."

They were silent. Time crawled along. Geir began to doze again. When nothing happened for a time, he found he could not keep his eyes open. But if the fire sparked a little or one of the wolves growled, he opened his eyes and stared into the darkness.

Suddenly they heard something scraping almost inaudibly against the big stone at the back of the hut. Immediately afterwards the snow on the top of the roof creaked and the walls trembled slightly. They also noticed that the pack outside was excited and very restless. The ring closed in, and several dark shadows ventured inside the circle of light between the fence and the fire.

This acted as a starter on Geir. He flew up, threw himself on his knees halfway out of the door, and almost without thinking took a handful of glowing embers from the fire and, exerting all his strength, threw this shower of fire high into the air. They heard a furious bark behind them, and the hut trembled and shook so violently that they expected both the wolf and the hut to come down on top of them at any moment.

Most of the embers landed on Geir himself when they fell down again, and he sprang up and danced a war dance to shake them off. Uncontrolled rage seized him, and it was as if he had lost his reason. He pulled out a burning branch from the fire and rushed forward to the fence of branches, jumped over it, and stamped forward a few steps in the loose snow until he stumbled and fell on his face. The branch sizzled in the snow and went out.

"Geir—are you mad—come back!" yelled Peter behind him.

Actually Geir had received a cold douche when he stumbled and fell. He now thought clearly and sanely again and knew as well as Peter that he must get back as quickly as he could. But it was more easily said than done. He struggled madly to get a foothold, but when he eventually got to his feet, he was in the snow up to his waist and could not turn round.

He glimpsed a shadow passing him like lightning. It was almost dark where he stood. He had a panicky feeling that there was a wolf just behind him and turned round so quickly that he almost fell again. But no sooner had he done this than he realized that he had turned his back on the pack and that they stood ready to spring in the darkness behind. He could hear them, but he could not see them. He struggled despairingly to get his face toward them again. Could he go backwards? He tried but gave it up. He glimpsed movements in the darkness and heard quick, excited breathing.

Then there was a shot from the hut. A signal bullet whistled close by his ear and landed with a frizzle in the snow.

"Come on!" He heard Peter's voice, unusually authoritative. "Hurry! I'll load as quickly as I can. Crawl!"

Geir threw himself down and crawled on all fours toward the branch fence.

Bang! A new shot went over his head. He reached the fence just as the third shot was fired. He broke through the fence and a moment later he sat breathless beside Peter in the hut. Everything had happened so quickly that they had scarcely taken it in before it was all over.

A little shamefacedly Geir opened his hand and looked at the burn. It was smarting tremendously and smelled of burned flesh, but it did not look as bad as he had expected.

Peter tore off a piece of parachute silk and bound him up.

"Thank you," said Geir, in a low voice without looking at him, "—for everything."

Peter did not answer. He looked at Geir in a surprised sort of way and then turned aside with a gleam in his eye.

"We'll laugh at this later on," he thought. "When all this is over, we'll think it dreadfully funny, but just now there is nothing amusing in it at all."

The wolves kept away for a long time. One of them howled once or twice, but the others did not answer, so that silence reigned. They might be a hundred yards away, or so the two fliers reckoned.

Geir lay on his back gazing up at the roof with no expression in his face at all, as if he had forgotten that the wolves existed. Peter kept watch. He sat up straight and kept his eye on the door, and in order to see better, he shaded his face from the fire with one hand.

While he was sitting like that, he became suddenly conscious of a little star just above the horizon.

"Geir!" He shouted so loudly that Geir jumped up and rushed to the door. He thought that the wolves had come back again. "Look!" cried Peter, and pointed. "It's clearing."

"It is, it is," whispered Geir. "Listen, the wind has dropped entirely. It's dead still, and colder!"

Involuntarily they both looked at their watches. It was a quarter to five.

"If this is not a false alarm," said Geir, "if really clear weather can be expected, the boys will be up and the planes will be out and flying at top speed. We can expect them here in a few hours."

Peter nodded. He moved his eyes from the twinkling point in the heavens to two smaller ones near the ground.

"They'll have to look nippy," he said, "for here come the beasts again!"

Twelve — The Jets Go Up

Ruste sat bent over a map, his head resting in his hands. His eyes were shut. Now and again his head slipped out of his hands and bowed politely down toward the table. Then he would fix his dry, red-rimmed eyes on the map again, but a moment or two later his eyelids inevitably closed and his breathing became heavy and regular. It was nighttime in the office of the Air Rescue Service, and the Chief Air Traffic Controller was sitting in a corner keeping an eye on the coffee kettle, which stood on a hot plate and was just beginning to boil.

Ruste had almost reached the end of his tether. It was more than forty-eight hours since he had been to bed, and before that his hours on duty had been as long, if not longer. It seemed to him as if this particular rescue operation had been going on forever and was more exacting than any other operation he could remember. The tragedy was that so little had been achieved, and nothing wears a man down more than repeated disappointments, unsuccessful attempts, followed by broodings over what had gone wrong, endless waiting for possible flying weather, depressing reports from the patrols and helicopters, and misleading information from people who said they had seen lights and signals in the most improbable places. More and more problems were piling up, and nothing leading to any concrete results.

Now he was worn out and tired, and his courage was beginning to run low.

The Chief Air Traffic Controller poured out two cups of coffee and brought one over to Ruste's desk.

"Why don't you go home and sleep?" he said. "You'll not find any solution by sitting there staring at the map until you break down completely."

Ruste gulped down the coffee, which livened him up a little. He followed the Air Traffic Controller back to his table in the corner and was given another cup of coffee. The Air Traffic Controller offered him a cigarette, and they each lit one.

"I'm not so sure of that," said Ruste. He was answering what the Air Traffic Controller had said a few minutes ago.

"If nothing else turns up, the map is our only chance. I have flown that route in my thoughts over and over again, have sat in the cockpit with the map on my knee, taken off from Bardufoss, planned the course and the height, weighed up the weather report, gone up through the clouds, announced my position, and jumped. I've got a hundred different positions, but none so far from the one the boys gave that it could make any great difference—except one. And I found that last night."

He fetched the map and kept his finger on a certain point.

"They gave their position as being here before they rose above the clouds. This was the last they saw of the ground, this lake, this river, this road—at least so they said."

"Y-ee-s. There could not have been much to go wrong with in that," said the Air Traffic Controller. "Why do you add 'so they said'?"

Ruste threw up his hands. "Anyone can make a mistake," he said. "Quite reliable people do. Among other things, the district police officer up there is quite certain that it was snowing heavily when the boys gave their position. It's more than easy to make a mistake when one only gets glimpses of the ground, and they had been flying in snow for a good while before they decided to rise."

Ruste picked up a pencil and drew a ring round the position the boys had given. Then he ringed a position about sixteen miles farther south. He said nothing.

The Air Traffic Controller gazed at the map for a long time in silence. "But of course," he said at last in a surprised tone of voice. "It's strange how similar the two positions look—at any rate on the map. I think possibly you are right."

"In that case it now moves our search area twenty-eight miles to the south," said Ruste, "as we moved it about twelve miles to the north the day before yesterday when we guessed that they had set their course for Alta as soon as the engine began to stall. I never thought much of that theory as they had not reported that they had changed course, but we had to try it when there was no trace of them in the first area."

He stubbed out his cigarette and tapped nervously on the table. "I ought to have thought of this before," he said, biting his lips.

"Nonsense," said the Air Traffic Controller. "As long as the flying weather is as bad as it has been, nothing can make much difference. We cannot overcome all difficulties. The area in which we have been searching is on the whole just as likely to be right as the one you mention, and the patrols and helicopters have not been able to cover the whole even now!"

"No, I realize that," said Ruste. "They need another day. We must clear up the one before we go over to the other, so we will let them keep on with the first plan tomorrow. But if there is no result, we have at any rate a new hope. I get furious when I think how simple everything would have been if we had had decent flying weather. Neither patrols nor helicopters can search efficiently as long as clouds cover the tops of the mountains. A mistake would be too costly. One scarcely knows what's best to do."

The Air Traffic Controller sighed deeply and poured out some more coffee.

"You're doing a good deal more than you ought to do," he said. "Who in the world could guard against mistakes in such a situation as this? If some idiot sees a star at Karasjok and thinks it's a lantern out on the moors, what can you do? Send a helicopter there? If nothing is found, then it was a mistake to take the plane away from the other area it was searching. But if you do not send it there and it is later confirmed that it really was a lantern—then *that* is a mistake. If you are trying to find a needle in a haystack, is it best to start at the bottom or the top? It depends where the needle is. Go home and get a little sleep. The greatest mistake is to wear yourself out. When flying weather finally comes, you'll not be in a fit state to use it to the best advantage."

Ruste said nothing. He rubbed his forehead thoughtfully and emptied his coffee cup in one gulp.

"Perhaps you're right," he said. "I think I'll go off home. You must get the plan going as soon as it is light."

Then the telephone rang.

Ruste sat down at his desk and lifted the receiver. "Air Rescue Service," he said heavily.

"Air Weather Office here," said a voice. "You can go all out now, Ruste. You'll have clear weather over the moors and over most of north Norway in three or four hours' time."

Ruste sprang out of his chair.

"Is that true?" he almost shouted. "Is that really true? I'll be with you in a few seconds. No wait, I must ring the Operations Room first."

He threw back the receiver onto the telephone, picked it up again, and dialed a new number. A moment later the Operations officer on duty answered him.

"Listen here," said Ruste. "It's clearing on the moors. Operation PLANESEARCH must go into action at once. All available planes must get up into the air. You have the Colonel's instructions and the list of those who are to take over. Give the alarm. The air crews are to meet me in the Operations Room in an hour's time."

He looked at the clock—half-past four exactly.

Ten seconds later Ruste was in the Air Weather Office bending over the meteorological chart.

Fifty seconds later a light appeared in a window in the station—then one more, then another. The silence was broken by the ringing of telephones, men shouting to each other, doors banging. Light after light went on, and the outlines of huts and buildings appeared in the darkness.

Five minutes later the telephone rang in the Operations Room at Bardufoss, and a minute later at Skattöra. There was feverish activity everywhere. From the mess came the noise of rattling china and cooking utensils. The pilots came running out of the doors with half their clothes over their arms. They stopped and looked up at the sky, nodded to each other, and started for the mess. The technicians went straight to the hangars; jeeps came rushing round corners. The heavy doors of the hangars creaked and rattled. Tractors started up and went in and out of the hangars, dragging planes out and returning empty. Propellers began to whir, and the first howls from the jet engine cut through the air.

At five o'clock the windows and walls were shaking from the noise of humming engines.

A little later the air crews were all in their places in the Operations Room. They knew what it was all about. Operation PLANESEARCH had already been gone through and planned. All orders had been given some days ago and each pilot knew the part he had to play. They had only been waiting for the moment when it would be possible to put the plan into action.

But Ruste had made one or two small alterations. He

had dictated them over the telephone to the Operations Officers at Bardufoss and Skattöra. In Bodö he was going to give them to the pilots himself.

When the Operations Officer told him to go ahead, he began by a short summary of all that had happened up to that moment and repeated the chief points in the plan for the day. Then he told the men of the new theory that he had worked out as he had sat staring at the map during the night.

He noticed that several of the pilots shook their heads skeptically, but as he talked on, explaining himself in more detail and pointing out the positions on the map, their faces grew interested and excited. They looked at each other and exchanged words and signs with those next to them. All knew how easy it was to make a mistake in snowy weather and bad visibility. Ruste's idea was not so improbable after all. It was worthwhile looking into it more closely anyhow.

Ruste finished all he had to say, left the platform, and sat down among the boys on the front bench. The Operations Officer began:

"On the whole we will follow the plan already worked out for operation PLANESEARCH," he said. "The helicopter and ground patrol will continue to search the areas they have been given. The Otter and the Norseman will search for the plane itself. All the jets, except four, will search the large area that is marked on the map from six miles south of Alta to nine miles north of Kautokeino. Every Flight Captain has been assigned a search area in the southern part on their way to the east and in the northern part on their way home. The formation will fly in line at 8,000 feet with a distance of three-quarters of a mile between the planes. Each man will search his area two miles to starboard of his own plane, so that the whole area will be doubly covered. Keep a lookout principally for signal rockets. The height and speed do not give you much chance of seeing anything else."

The Operations Officer paused and asked if there were any questions. His eyes passed along the lines of eager faces, but as no one held up his hand, he went on.

"Panther Red, who will actually be flying farthest south, will be given a special task. You will land at Bardufoss and refuel so that you can search at a lower level and stay longer in the search area than the others. You will search the new area that has been suggested because the pilots' last known position may have been wrong. You will be given more detailed orders later on."

After the Weather Officer had given information about the weather and the signal officer about the radio frequencies to be used, Ruste spoke once more.

"So far we have been unlucky in this rescue operation," he said. "The weather has stopped us getting down to it properly, and it has been heart-rending to imagine what those two boys have had to go through while we have been sitting here with our hands in our laps, so to speak. But don't be discouraged. There is no reason to believe that they have not managed all right. Lieutenant Grand knows the moors and has been up there for a winter course. He knows how to keep going in the North. There are fish in practically every lake and river, and it is quite possible to snare birds and other small game. You must never for one moment doubt that it is worthwhile hunting. With the additional search area we are including today, we have every chance of finding them—and saving them. Good luck to you all!"

The pilots rose and pressed eagerly toward the door. A few minutes later Ruste stood there alone as the door banged after the last man. The square in front hummed with impatient voices shouting orders. Cars started up and disappeared. Then all was quiet. Only then did Ruste notice that the noise of engines had stopped. The planes were warmed up and inspected. They were ready to start.

He lit a cigarette and stood absent-mindedly gazing at the map of the Finnmark Moors. Then he turned slowly on his heels and walked heavily toward the door.

There was nothing more that he could do.

Thirteen — At Last

When the first streak of dawn showed above the horizon, Geir and Peter were so tired that their eyelids closed and they dozed off. Geir slept restlessly, throwing himself back and forth, and his eyes had half opened several times before he was able finally to drag himself right out of sleep.

Then he suddenly sat bolt upright. A clear blue sky showed through the door opening.

His fatigue disappeared as if blown away by a strong wind. He put on his boots and cooked breakfast, a trout each. Then he woke Peter.

"There isn't a cloud in the sky. We shall have half the Air Force over us within half an hour," he cried.

They were both excited and impatient. After breakfast Geir could not sit still. He pottered round the hut, gazing up into the sky in all directions. Finally he began to shiver.

"I think I'll go and see to the snares and get more wood," he said. "If we've got any ptarmigans, we can always take them home with us and sell them in the market."

Peter smiled. He had an expectant, sucking feeling in

his stomach. He, also, found it difficult to keep still, but he, of course, was tied to his dinghy.

When Geir had examined the snares, he hung his leather jacket and the signal pistol in a tree and began to cut up wood with an eagerness caused by impatience rather than by any real necessity. They had plenty of wood for the present, and he might well have postponed cutting any more until the next day—if such a dreadful thing should happen as their not being found today.

He had just cut up a small birch tree and was well on his way with another when he suddenly stopped, stood stock still, and listened. A vibrating sound in the air, almost inaudible, reached his ears. It was a sound he knew too well to mistake.

"Peter!" he yelled at the top of his voice. "They're coming! Jets!"

He did not give himself time to listen again but began to run out of the wood onto open ground. Then he remembered that he had left the signal pistol hanging in the tree. He stopped so suddenly that he lost his balance and fell down head foremost, and one of his snowshoes fell off. It cost him many precious seconds to get onto his feet again. Meanwhile, the drone of engines grew stronger as the planes came quickly nearer, and while he hobbled and crawled back up the hill with his snowshoe in his hand, he was almost crying with vexation. He heard from the sound that his chance of reaching the pistol before the planes were just above him was very small, especially as he would have to load before he could shoot. No—it was hopeless. It was useless to hurry. He might as well give up at once.

He stopped breathless and stared despairingly at the four jets flying eastwards at a great height. Although he knew that they were too high to see him there in the little wood, he waved madly with his cap in one hand and his loose snowshoe in the other.

Suddenly he heard a bang from down by the hut, and two red lights rose heavenward.

A feeling of great warmth went through him. Peter had made it. He who was tied down to his dinghy had been quick enough both in thought and action to do what was necessary.

The planes were almost on a level with the camp when the rocket went off, and Geir followed them with his eyes in almost breathless suspense. But not one of them showed any sign of altering its course. They continued straight on, growing smaller and smaller until the drone of the engines died slowly away.

Geir's body felt quite numb, and his disappointment was followed by qualms of conscience. He dreaded to go down and explain to Peter why he had not fired. He also felt as if he had failed the pilots who had passed them. Those boys up there were perhaps friends of his who were taking a risk by paying less attention to the actual flying in order to search the ground beneath them. Now they were staring at an empty landscape and had no idea that they had just flown past the point for which they were searching. They were searching in vain—because he had been fooling about.

Then he pulled himself together and hurried down to the hut, where he found Peter lying on his stomach in the door opening. His feet were still wrapped up in the parachute silk.

"I'm beginning to think that we shall be spending Midsummer Day* here," said Peter, smiling courageously, "so I had a try to see that the fireworks were in order."

"You're pale," said Geir quickly. "Have you twisted your leg?"

"A bit I think. I didn't get out of the dinghy quickly enough. There seemed to be at least a hundred thousand layers of silk."

He groaned a little when Geir lifted him back into the dinghy. The splints were considerably out of place, and Geir began at once to straighten them out.

"I'm afraid you have broken it again," he said. "I expect it had begun to grow. How does it feel?"

"Splendid, thank you," said Peter. His hair was wet with perspiration.

Geir cleared his throat. "It was my fault," he said thickly. "I hung the pistol up in a tree, stumbled in my hurry when I went to fetch it, and lay in the snow crawling about like an idiot."

He went out backwards through the door and hung about buttoning up his jacket.

"Pity you did it in vain," he said.

He went to fetch the signal pistol and did not hear what Peter answered.

There was a trout on the line, and Geir cooked it for

* Midsummer Day, June 24th, is a great day in the Scandinavian countries and is celebrated with fireworks and other festivities.

lunch at half-past ten. The atmosphere was more than gloomy. Their disappointment increased and hope diminished as the time passed. A few clouds appeared in the west, and Geir kept an anxious eye fixed on them. It was true they were very high and looked quite harmless, but one can never tell what will develop.

Peter tried to keep up their spirits.

"We shall have them back again in a few hours," he insisted. "They're just filling up at Bardufoss—and then they'll come back."

"Yes, they'll come back sooner or later, I have no doubt," said Geir. "But perhaps they've another area to search first, and we can't be sure that they'll start a fresh round today or whether the clouds will not lie low again."

"If that happens, it will be crazy for you to stay here any longer," said Peter. "You must go off and find civilization."

"Don't be ridiculous," said Geir. "How do you propose to get on alone?"

Peter thought for a moment.

"Listen to me," he said. "If you go northwards, you will strike some valley or other that will lead you toward the coast. The sea cannot be far off. You can reckon on getting there within a couple of days. It is more than likely that the ski patrols have been hunting for us in the north and that you will find their ski tracks. You can cook all the food we can get hold of and leave part of it here for me. Then you can wall up the door . . ."

He got no further.

"Shs-s-s!" said Geir. His quick ear had caught the

weak, trembling note in the air again, the sound of an engine far, far away. He caught up the signal pistol and leaped to the door. In his haste he caught his foot in the parachute and tumbled head first halfway out of the door. A big lump of snow fell out of the wall and hit him on the shoulders. He kicked and wriggled himself free, flinging his arms about to shake off the snow. The transition from calm to wild chaos was so overwhelming that Peter laughed loudly, tensed up as he was.

No sooner was Geir on his feet again than he came crawling back on all fours and snatched up two signal cartridges. He edged himself backwards out of the hut again and took with him another piece of the wall. This time it was Peter who received the shower of snow as he had shuffled himself forward almost to the door.

Geir stopped beside the fire. The sound had become a little stronger and rose and fell for a time. Then it grew into an even monotone and quickly increased in strength.

Geir gazed at the horizon from south to north while he was putting a cartridge into the pistol. There—just over the horizon, he saw a dark point clearly marked against the sky. It quickly grew larger.

Bang—! Geir fired the first shot and then loaded again while the red ball of fire rose in a high arc fifty yards or so into the air. He could already distinguish the shape of a plane. It was flying low, about 3,000-4,000 feet. He saw another a little farther to the south, but the nearest one looked as if it were taking a course rather too far south of the camp. That meant that the pilot would not see them if he were looking to starboard when the shots went up.

Geir's hand shook. He fired another shot, but the plane continued steadily on its course.

"Another cartridge, Peter, quick!" he said, kneeling at the entrance and holding out his hand backwards into the hut. "Hurry up!" he shouted impatiently.

At that very moment he heard a new and sharper sound above him. He turned sharply and saw a third plane coming in almost directly from the west, making straight for them. It was on its way down in a shallow dive. There could be no doubt—they had been found.

Geir gave a roar and danced a war dance around the fire. He waved his arms and legs and shouted excitedly. "He sees us! He sees us!"

The jet approached them at great speed. It was down to between 70 and 80 feet, about halfway out on the ice, and came toward them like a projectile. The noise of its jet engine rose to a roar, making the air tremble as the plane rushed past and rose perpendicularly above them. At the top it went into a roll and then swung round the camp.

Geir pulled Peter in his dinghy out of the hut. Half the wall fell down, and Peter was covered with snow, but he only laughed. Both of them shouted and laughed and waved wildly to the pilot in the cockpit, who waved back to them almost as wildly.

A few minutes later three other planes came in from the south in close formation. The first went to meet them and joined the formation and all four continued to circle round the camp.

"Now they're sending information home via Alta," said Geir.

"Yes—at last," said Peter with a sigh.

Then he laughed. "But look at them now," he said. "Have you ever seen such an untidy formation. A disgrace to the Norwegian Air Force!"

Fourteen — A Message for Svein

"Panther Leader from Red Four. Signal lights straight in front of me—about four miles. Over."

The pilot who had discovered the boys leaned excitedly to one side and put the stick over in order to see better. A moment later he saw another light flickering across the snow and caught sight of a tiny speck moving on the ground. An enthusiastically eager voice came in over the radio. It was the Squadron Leader.

"Well done, Red Four. Go down and investigate. Red, two and three, close formation."

Red Four dived toward the camp. He heard the Squadron Leader give the announcement to all stations and planes, telling them to stand by for more detailed information.

"In a few seconds," he thought, "the announcement will go out over the telephone and telegraph wires. In a few minutes they will know in Oslo what has happened here on the Finnmark Moors. The radio will break off the regular program and the whole country will know that they are alive—or, at any rate, one."

He was now so low that the camp disappeared beneath

the nose of his plane. Not until he had risen and was circling them could he see them clearly and know they were both alive.

"It looks as if one of them is injured," he announced. "But he is sitting in the dinghy and waving both his arms."

"O.K. We'll be with you in a moment. Join the formation," said the Panther Leader. They circled over the boys for twenty minutes and sent information about all they could see. Telegraph clerk Berntsen, in Alta, hummed contentedly and sent on all the messages. The boys had never been out of his thoughts for a moment since he had spoken to them before they jumped.

The first announcements reached the Air Rescue Coordination Center just before a new jet squadron was about to take off to relieve the first one. Some of them were already on their way to the runway when they were ordered back to the hangars. Lieutenant Colonel Ruste gave a long sigh of relief. "Take over," he said to the Chief Air Traffic Controller. "I'm going to have a sleep in my office. Wake me when they are on board the helicopter." Then he wandered off into his office, sat down at his desk, put his head on his arms, and fell asleep immediately.

While all this was happening, Svein was flying low, hunting for the boys in a little valley. The Panther Leader called him time and time again, but the helicopter was shielded by the sides of the valley so that the call did not reach him. Therefore, Svein was one of the last to hear that the boys were found.

He sat in his helicopter gazing at the ground below him,

entirely dispirited. His technician drew his attention to the fact that they must soon get back to Kautokeino to fill up with gasoline—for the second time that day—and again he had not accomplished what he had set out to do. The hope that had flared up in the morning when the announcement about clear weather had come through was receding again. There was no sign of life anywhere, and he would soon have explored the search area from end to end. If the boys were not very far from the area that the Air Rescue Service considered probable, they must be well hidden and quite unable to make any sort of contact—perhaps buried in the snow.

He shook off this gloomy thought and descended even lower to make sure he had not missed any details in the forest-clad valley.

When he came out of the valley, he rose higher and by chance picked up a word or two at the end of a radio announcement. This gave him the impression that something was in the wind, so he shouted eagerly, "All planes, this is Helicopter One Four. Have you any news? Over."

He heard a relieved voice, which answered immediately.

"Helicopter One Four. This is Panther. The pilots have been found in position 69 ° 24′ North, 23 ° 12′ East. Over."

Svein glanced uncertainly at his technician. The blood rushed to his face and he began to tremble.

"Panther," he said thickly, "are they alive?"

"Yes, one of them is injured, but it does not look to be very serious."

Svein's voice returned to its usual form. It resounded so loudly in the ether that the pilots in the eight or ten planes jumped in their seats.

"Thank you, Panther. I'll go straight to Kautokeino and fill up. I'll start from there in under an hour. One Four out."

He revved up the engine. The helicopter rocked but increased its speed. Both Svein and the technician leaned far forward in the cockpit as if hoping that this would help.

"How far are they from Kautokeino?" asked Svein.

"Half an hour's flying I should think," said the technician as he glanced at the map. "Wait a moment and I'll work it out more exactly."

He measured with his thumb and first finger and studied the map for a time, a frown between his eyes.

"Yes—that's right," he said at last. "Half an hour. But I say, that's queer. You remember the area they mentioned this morning for a special search? That's where they are. Why didn't they give us that job?"

Svein shook his head. "The ways of the Air Rescue Service are past finding out," he said, "but they're not generally as stupid as they seem. I imagine that probably the boys were not where they were supposed to be, but somewhere quite different."

The technician gave him an inquiring look. Then he shrugged his shoulders and lapsed into silence.

In Kautokeino everything was in readiness to have the helicopter serviced and off again as quickly as possible. The gasoline was brought right up to the landing place, and four or five soldiers stood ready to help the technician to fill up and to mount the stretcher. Svein walked impatiently up and down, smoking a cigarette, throwing the stub away and lighting a new one. He had a map in his hand but did not give himself time to study it. Once or twice he put out his cigarette and came nearer to see if there was something he could do to help, but the technician was seeing to everything and it did not look as if any detail had been forgotten. A soldier rushed up with a packet of sandwiches and three Thermos bottles full of coffee, which were all stowed away in the cockpit. Another loaded blankets and an extra first-aid box onto the stretcher.

Svein, therefore, saw no reason to take part in what was going on and tried to control his eagerness until the technician beckoned him and told him all was in order.

Then he almost ran to the cockpit, fastened himself in, and signed to the technician, who waved the soldiers aside and went and stood a few yards in front of the helicopter.

"Contact?"

The technician nodded. "Contact!"

Svein pushed in the self-starter.

The engine was still warm, so he was able to go all out straight away. The helicopter rose with a jerk to almost eight feet, where it remained stationary for a moment in the midst of a veritable storm of snow whirled up by the pressure of the air. Svein nodded good-by to his technician, pushed the stick forward, moved onward a few yards, and then rose in a steep angle toward the north.

At last he was really on his way.

He kept the engine in top gear and climbed as quickly as possible. He wanted to get as high as he could to get a good view all round him. Although it was much too early to be able to see anything concrete, he gazed eagerly northward. Great snow-covered plains and low mountain ridges lay before him. Somewhere behind those ridges the boys were waiting and listening for the sound of an engine. He wanted to get so high that they should not be in suspense for a single moment longer than was necessary—neither they nor he, for that matter.

He hummed softly to himself, and it would have seemed strange if he had not done so, for everybody knew that Svein sang while he flew, although no one had ever heard a note from him on the ground. He always said he had a microphone voice and that down on the ground he left all music to the radio and the phonograph, but he sang all the more when he was in the air. Now and again he forgot himself when he pressed the button to send out a message or a report and a bar or two floated out into the ether. These "wireless programs" from Helicopter One Four were a welcome distraction to the other pilots, and they smiled at them indulgently and joked about them when they landed.

After flying for about a quarter of an hour, Svein looked at his watch and began to hurry more than ever. His grip on the stick became firmer, and he swallowed hard once or twice. His eyes wandered restlessly from side to side. They ought soon to be able to hear him. He could expect a signal from the ground at any moment.

A minute passed; then a green signal light rose into the air six or seven miles away.

Although he had been waiting for it, he gave such a start when he saw it that he nearly jumped out of his seat. In his eagerness to get a glimpse of the boys, he leaned forward so quickly that he almost knocked his chin against the stick.

"You old fool," he murmured. "I didn't know you could be such an idiot."

He shook the stick and waved with the whole plane. The plane swung to and fro in sudden slalom twists until the rotor blades knocked together in a sinister manner. By now he could see a blue trail of smoke from a fire and a dark spot that might be one of the boys. When he got the helicopter onto a straight course again, he called up Alta and reported that he was in contact with the two pilots and would be landing in a few minutes. Then he pushed the stick forward and went into a shallow glide toward the camp. His speed increased, and the dark spot began to take form. It was a brown leather jacket in incessant motion. It seemed to be dancing backwards and forwards in jerks and leaps, waving its arms up and down like a jumping jack.

Svein threw back his head and laughed.

"This must be dead against all tradition," he murmured. "When ordinary folk in distress are rescued, they generally use their last ounce of strength to lift a hand in greeting before sinking back into unconsciousness. It must be quite unique for those who are about to be rescued to welcome their rescuers with an exhibition of acrobatic dancing."

Fifteen — Farewell to the Wilderness

Geir lowered the pistol. He had seen the helicopter like a spot against the blue sky. It was rolling forward in mad antics, and he knew what that meant. There was no need to shoot any more. In a few moments the solitary life in the wilderness would be ended.

He turned round and looked at Peter, who was following all that was happening from the door. Neither of them said anything. This was not the moment for shouting and wild enthusiasm. They both had a lump in their throats, which must be swallowed before they could give expression to what they felt.

Geir kicked a little snow onto the campfire to make it smoke more strongly, but that was scarcely necessary, for the pilot in the helicopter could apparently see them already. But there was no harm in doing it, and he felt like a little movement.

The noise of the engines increased. They could distinguish the yellow floats and the plastic cockpit and could glimpse the pilot like a shadow behind the Plexiglas. The helicopter was on its way down and was making good speed.

"I think it's Svein," cried Geir. "It can't be anyone else with his head almost hitting the ceiling of the cockpit."

Suddenly he changed entirely, and both movement and speech came back to him. He jumped high into the air and waved his arms wildly.

"Prepare for a tremendous scolding, Peter," he said with a laugh. "We are sure to have robbed him of many hours of sleep!"

By now the helicopter had come so near that they could see Svein waving to them. They no longer doubted that it was he. Geir rushed into the hut and tore off a long strip of parachute silk and, fastening it to a little branch, hurried down onto the ice. When Svein swung above them, Geir held the branch high into the air and the silk strip waved in the weak breeze, showing Svein in what direction the wind was coming.

The noise of the engines stopped, and the clattering of the rotor grew stronger. The helicopter sank quickly toward the ground. It made a sharp swing out over the lake and came gliding up against the wind. When it was some feet above the ground, the engine began to work at full strength again, and a whirl of wind and snow and noise surrounded Geir so that he was obliged to bend down and turn his back to it. Then suddenly the noise of the engine stopped and the sound of the rotor became weaker and weaker.

Geir turned round and saw Svein opening the cockpit door. His reverberating voice was almost a shock in the sudden stillness, saying, "Are you flesh and blood or are you a ghost?"

Geir swallowed. He saw Svein jump out of the cockpit and sink up to his knees in the snow.

"Touch me and see!" he said, clearing his voice. He bent down under the whirling rotor and went up to Svein. They were almost on a level—Geir on his snowshoes and Svein without them.

Svein took hold of Geir by the shoulders and shook him. "You're real enough," he said. "Are you sound and well also?"

"Yes."

"And your stable companion?"

"He broke his leg when landing. Otherwise he's all right."

Svein shook his head skeptically.

"May I be so free as to ask what you are living on?"

"Hunting and fishing. We've got two ptarmigan and four trout to take home with us. We live in a warm and comfortable hut and eat four meals a day."

"Fine. Half the Air Force and all Air Rescue Service are nervous wrecks. While we all suffer tortures and risk our lives and our health to find you, the two of you have been having a good holiday on full pay and making extra by hunting and fishing. It wouldn't surprise me if you landed a job as a reindeer hunter, too!"

"No, our domestic animals do not allow themselves to be hunted," said Geir. "They hunt us."

They were interrupted by Peter's impatient voice from the hut. His fair head popped up beside the heap of smoke from the campfire. "Hello," he shouted.

"Hello!" answered Svein. "Mr. Hovden, I presume?"

"Rightly guessed," came the answer from above. "When you have finished embracing each other, perhaps you will take a little walk up here and say how do you do to me."

"We'll be with you in a moment," said Svein. "Put on the coffee."

He went back into the cockpit, pulled out a pair of snowshoes, and put them on.

"I have one or two meager sandwiches with me and a little coffee," he said. "I don't know if that attracts you at all."

"Oh, yes," said Geir with a laugh. "A little change in our diet will be quite welcome."

They walked together up to the hut.

"Your mother asked me to give you her love," said Svein. "I have rung her once or twice—last night was the latest."

"How did she take it?"

"Tja—she was a little bit difficult to convince. Imagination runs away with her now and again, but you know her better than I do."

"And everything's all right otherwise—with the family, I mean?"

"Fine. I expect they have already killed the fatted calf—"

He stopped and threw a sidelong look at Geir and lowered his voice. "They'll have had a report by now. You can imagine how happy they will be to know that you have been found and that you are alive."

They were halfway up the little hill when Svein suddenly stopped and stared at tracks in the snow.

"Have you a dog?" he asked, surprised.

"Wolves," said Geir.

"Nonsense. Wolves so near the hut? Nonsense!"

"Look about you," said Geir. "There are tracks everywhere. Eight to ten thin, desperate beasts have disturbed us for the last two nights."

"My goodness, that is the sort of thing one imagines happens only in books, and in olden days too—not now."

"I thought the same," said Geir, "but wolves are just as hungry now as they were then, and when their hunger becomes strong enough, they return to their old habits."

"I think you're crazy," said Svein uncertainly. He paused and took a walk round, looking about him all the time. "It must be true," he murmured. "Where are they now?"

Geir shrugged his shoulders. "Don't ask me," he said. "They stay away the whole day and come back as soon as it gets dark, more hungry and more insistent every night. I think it was just about time you found us."

"I think so, too," said Peter's impatient voice from the hut. They had come so near that he could hear what they were saying. "But it doesn't look as if *I* am going to be rescued even now," he added.

"In one moment," answered Svein. "There's an old custom that we all subscribe to, namely, that we rescue those men who are fit and able-bodied first because they increase the country's output."

When they reached him, Svein squeezed Peter's hand and lifted him back into his dinghy so that there was room for all three of them in the hut. He was very impressed by the camp and the way in which they had settled themselves in, and he asked again and again, while he was opening the food packets and handing round sandwiches and coffee, how they had managed to carry on.

Geir and Peter set to. It looked as if they had not tasted food for a long time, and Geir thought that their appetites needed an explanation.

"It's because there is salt in the sandwiches," he said.

"That's right," said Peter. "I've just decided to eat half a pound of salt the moment I get home."

"Right you are," said Svein. "I'll personally see that you are given it when we get to Kautokeino in an hour's time, but if both of you will finish the sandwiches, we can get off before the engines get too cold."

"There are only three left," said Geir, "and I don't feel I can eat any more. I am ready when you are."

"Me, too," said Peter.

Then they got up and left everything they did not actually need in the camp. Svein dragged Peter in the dinghy toward the helicopter. Geir took a short cut to the fishing place and pulled up the net. There were two wriggling trout in it. He wetted his hand in the water, released them carefully, and put them back in the lake. When he reached the plane, Svein had lifted the lid from the stretcher and was waiting for his help to lift Peter into it.

"Were there any fish?" he asked.

Geir nodded. "Two. That line could have caught a hundred if I had left it. I took in the snares as soon as the jets had been here. Now we'll be leaving the animals in peace, in gratitude to them for giving us what we needed while we were here."

They settled Peter down, packing him in with blankets, and securing the lid over him. Then they went into the cockpit and fastened themselves in. Geir took his snowshoes with him. He wanted to keep them as a memento.

Three minutes later they were in the air. Svein swung round the camp and then set a course toward the south.

"An Otter is waiting for you in Kautokeino," he said. "You'll be eating your dinner in Bodö."

Geir leaned against the Plexiglas and looked back. Almost the whole area over which he had tottered in his snowshoes, in which he had worked and fought for life, and which had given him so many disappointments and joys, lay behind them, white and untouched, as if there had never been life there at all. Distance had wiped out the tracks. Suddenly it seemed to him that what they had lived through was like a rare dream. It all seemed entirely unreal. Now they were returning again to civilized life. In a few days, or at any rate a few weeks, he would again be sitting at his stick in the Otter and life would follow its usual course. All would be as before—not perhaps quite as before. Peter would not be sitting beside him, not for a long time at any rate.

He bent forward and looked in through the opening to the stretcher. Peter turned his pale face toward him and smiled.

With a sudden inspiration Geir gripped his hand and squeezed it hard. "Congratulations," he shouted above the noise of the engines. "Congratulations that we are saved. Now you must get well quickly. I'll hold the job open for you. We'll fly together again as soon as you're well."

Peter did not answer. He held Geir's hand tightly, as if he would never let it go.

Svein threw a quick glance at them, and an amused gleam appeared in the corner of his eye. He spoke to Geir through the microphone in a low voice. "I expect he was boasting when he talked about his table tennis," he said, "but we can soon teach him; he has a quick brain."

Then Geir knew that nothing would be quite as before. From now on there would be three where before there had been two.

He leaned back in the corner and shut his eyes. The helicopter glided evenly and quietly through the air, vibrating in its own particular lulling manner. It was delightful to relax and know that the responsibility had been taken over by someone else. Then very suddenly he started. A broad smile crossed his face and remained there. He arranged the earphones comfortably on his head and dozed off to the sound of Svein's singing.

Some Information about Planes and the Men Who Fly Them

An Air Force Station is a large concern where all activity is directed toward one aim and object alone—namely to keep the planes in the air. But only a small proportion of the people employed there are airmen. In our days the business of flying is too complicated to be one man's job. It is necessary that both pilots and a number of ground staff specialists shall work together as closely as the cogs in a cogwheel.

The Norwegian Station Commander controls all activity through the heads of three groups, each with their different spheres of action. The Operational Group deals with flying operations and exercises, the Technical Group is responsible for the maintenance and repair of the planes, and the Administrative Group deals with accounts, building operations, and catering.

The technicians work in the hangers and the workshops. Some are engineers, others specialists in the bodywork of the plane or in the instruments used in flying. The Communications Section deals with radio and radar. The depots store and hand out reserve parts and tools, while the Rescue Section packs parachutes and checks the pilots' safety equipment.

When the pilots are in the air, they are always in touch by radio with the Traffic Control in the Control Tower. This is a civil organization that is not subject to military control. The staff are called Air Traffic Controllers. They are the policemen of the air. By regulating the height and course of the planes, they see to it that no planes come into collision or get in each other's way.

The Air Weather Office gives them all information about weather conditions and is thus able to warn and advise all planes in the air.

The head of the Air Traffic Controllers is the Chief Controller of the area. He is responsible for the safety of civil and military air-traffic over a large area, which may include many airfields.

The Air Rescue Service is also attached to the Air Traffic Control. When a plane is missing or is wrecked, the Chief Controller gives the alarm, and a great rescue operation is set in motion. The airports do their part with rescue planes, helicopters, flying boats and patrols; the area police force collects voluntary helpers, the Red Cross units stand by, and the lifeboats all along the coast prepare for action. The whole operation follows a general plan prepared by the Air Traffic Control and Air Rescue Service.

Military flying divisions are called squadrons. A number of squadrons use transport planes, seaplanes, or helicopters, but most of them consist of modern fast-flying jet planes.

Some of the best-known types in the Norwegian Air Force are: (1) The jet plane "*Thunderjet*"; (2) the transport plane "*Otter*"; (3) the seaplane "*Norseman*"; and (4) the helicopter "*Bell 47*."

The *Thunderjet* is a single-seater jet with a top speed of 500 miles per hour.

The *Otter* is a one-engined passenger and ambulance plane carrying two airmen and eight passengers.

The *Norseman* resembles the Otter but has a rather smaller space for passengers and is fitted with floats.

Bell 47 is a three-seater helicopter, with both a main vertical rotor and a tail rotor. The main rotor acts both as wings and propeller. When it is horizontal, the helicopter ascends straight up from the ground, but by altering the setting, the pilot can get it to fly forwards, backwards, or sideways. The tail rotor keeps the fuselage steady in the air and prevents it from turning round on its own axis. For the transport of the sick, a stretcher is secured outside the body of the plane. It is closed but has a small opening into the cockpit.